"Is that what you're thinking? That I've been following you? Stalking you? You're the one who came to me, Scarlett. The one who needed me, and I helped you, no questions asked."

He had. He'd been there when she needed a friend most. But...he wasn't a friend.

He'd always been more.

He leaned nearer. Their bodies brushed. Their mouths were so close. The anger that had been between them was changing. Shifting. Becoming something else entirely.

"I knew for years..." His words were a rumble. "Knew I should stay away from you. If I ever got close again, I understood what would happen."

She didn't understand. "What would happen?"

His eyes were on her mouth. "This."

He lowered his head more, closed that last bit of precious distance between them and kissed her.

There were a million reasons why she should back away from him right then.

But her hands just rose up and curled around his shoulders to hold him tightly.

CONFESSIONS

New York Times Bestselling Author

—————

CYNTHIA EDEN

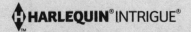
HARLEQUIN® INTRIGUE®

This book is for all of the wonderful readers who've written to me about my Harlequin Intrigue books. Thank you for your support! I hope you keep enjoying the stories!

ISBN-13: 978-0-373-69812-7

Confessions

Copyright © 2015 by Cindy Roussos

PLEASE RECYCLE

THIS PRODUCT IS RECYCLABLE

Recycling programs for this product may not exist in your area.

Printed in U.S.A.

HARLEQUIN®
www.Harlequin.com

Cynthia Eden, a *New York Times* bestselling author, writes tales of romantic suspense and paranormal romance. Her books have received starred reviews from *Publishers Weekly*, and she has received a RITA® Award nomination for best romantic suspense novel. Cynthia lives in the Deep South, loves horror movies and has an addiction to chocolate. More information about Cynthia may be found at cynthiaeden.com, or you can follow her on Twitter, @cynthiaeden.

Books by Cynthia Eden

Harlequin Intrigue

The Battling McGuire Boys series
Confessions

Shadow Agents series
Alpha One
Guardian Ranger
Sharpshooter
Glitter and Gunfire

Shadow Agents: Guts and Glory series
Undercover Captor
The Girl Next Door
Evidence of Passion
Way of the Shadows

Visit the Author Profile page at Harlequin.com for more titles.

CAST OF CHARACTERS

Grant McGuire—A ghost from Grant's past has just walked through his door. Former army ranger Grant is used to facing danger, but as he stares into the eyes of the only woman he ever loved—the woman he lost years ago—he knows that he may just be facing the toughest battle of his life.

Scarlett Stone—Scarlett didn't head into McGuire Securities because she wanted to relive the past. She's a desperate woman, and a desperate woman will do anything—even turn to the lover who broke her heart (or splintered it beneath his army boots). She is being framed for murder, and if Grant can't prove her innocence, she may just lose her freedom...and her life.

Justin Turner—Justin is convinced that Scarlett murdered his brother, and he won't rest until she gets the punishment she deserves. And if the law won't punish her, then he will. There is no way that Justin will let Scarlett get away from him...no matter what he has to do...

Shayne Townsend—Detective Townsend knows that there is more to Scarlett's case than meets the eye, but he has to follow orders and do his job. If he and Grant can't find evidence to clear Scarlett, then he will have to be the one to lock her away.

Sullivan McGuire—Sullivan knows all of Scarlett's secrets...secrets that even his brother Grant doesn't know. But when someone starts targeting Scarlett with a series of dangerous attacks, this ex-marine will stand by his brother's side in order to protect Scarlett. The McGuires always stand together...no matter how deadly the situation may be.

Prologue

"You're…leaving?" Scarlett Stone stared up at the man before her, aware that her heart was aching. Not aching…*breaking.*

"I have a new mission," Grant McGuire told her, his deep voice strangely devoid of its usual warmth. "I head out tomorrow and I don't know when I'll be back." The setting sun glinted off his blond hair. Grant… Tall, handsome, *perfect* Grant.

She'd graduated high school a few months ago. College awaited her. These days were supposed to be the start of a great new life. A new life she'd wanted to spend with him.

Grant was four years older than she was. Popular, confident, strong. He'd been in the army for the past few years, but he'd come to see her. Every time that he came home, he made certain he spent his days with her.

But he's leaving again now.

His hand lifted and his calloused fingertips slid over her cheek. His touch chased some of the chill from her skin. Strange. An August evening in Texas shouldn't have been cold…so why did she have goose bumps on her arms?

"You'll enjoy college," Grant told her in that low, rumbling voice that always made her stomach twist. "You'll have the time of your life there." His hand fell away from her. "But I need to head out again."

He was always leaving. "Why?"

"The ranch…this place isn't for me, Scarlett. I need more."

The place wasn't for him, but what about her? "Am I for you?" They'd started dating when she'd been a freshman in high school.

She'd been in love with him from the first moment she glanced up and saw him walking down the hallway. The senior…the quarterback…who'd shown interest in *her*.

When no one else ever had.

She was the nerd, the girl with her head always shoved in a book, too nervous to talk to boys. Someone most boys didn't notice.

But Grant had been different. Grant was always… different.

He was also not answering her.

"Grant?" Her hands lifted and pressed against his chest. "You know…I love you." It was the first time she'd ever confessed her true feelings to him, but surely he knew how she felt.

His muscles were hard beneath her palms. His green eyes stared down at her, but his gaze was shadowed, his emotions carefully hidden.

"I can wait for you to come back," she told him, and she knew her voice sounded desperate. "I don't mind waiting. I mean, my college break might happen right at the same time you get back, and I can wait—"

"Scarlett…"

Forever.

"I don't know when I'll be back." He brushed back her

hair, strands that the light breeze had shifted against her cheek. "And I don't want you to wait for me."

Pain knifed through her. "Grant?"

He leaned over her. His head bent, and his lips brushed against hers. She loved Grant's kiss. Loved the way he tasted. The way he made her feel.

Desired. Special.

A low moan built in her throat as he kissed her.

"You deserve to be happy," he whispered against her mouth. "I can't...I can't make you happy. I can't be who you want me to be."

What did that even mean? "I love you just as you are." She didn't want him to be anyone else.

But he shook his head. "Baby, you don't even know who I really am."

There had always been secrets in his eyes. A darkness that shadowed him. He'd been in the military for the past three years...and every time he'd come home, there had been a new hardness to him. A sharpening edge of danger.

"I can't tell you where I'm going, and I don't know when I'll be back. I won't ask you to wait for me." His forehead leaned against hers. "I can't."

Tears stung her eyes. She'd been dreaming of a new life—so many plans and dreams for the two of them. She wanted a new life with Grant, but...

"You have your scholarship," he continued, his voice sounding ragged, as emotion finally seemed to break through for him. "Take it. Take the life that's waiting for you."

Her hands lifted and curled around his shoulders. She knew a good-bye when she heard one. After all, she'd heard plenty of them in her life.

He kissed her again. There was desire and need in that kiss. She rose onto her toes, trying to get even closer to him. Scarlett wanted to be as close to him as she could get—

"I won't forget you," Grant told her.

He'd pulled away.

He always did.

She wrapped her arms around her stomach and blinked away the tears that wanted to fall.

"If you…if you ever need me…" His voice was gruff, shaking. Strange. He never sounded uncertain, but he did in that moment. "I'll be there for you, Scarlett."

She almost called him a liar. Because he was *leaving*. There was no way he could be there for her when he'd be gone.

But it hurt too much to talk anymore. She'd finally realized a painful truth.

I love him…but he doesn't love me.

Story of her life.

Scarlett stiffened her spine. She wouldn't reach out to him again. "Goodbye," she whispered, because there was no more to say. He hadn't invited her out here, to *their* spot by the lake, because he wanted to make plans about their future. He'd brought her out here to break up with her.

To leave her behind.

She turned away so he wouldn't see her crying. She took one step. Another.

Scarlett wouldn't let herself glance back. Grant McGuire was done with her. And she…she would be fine without him.

If you ever need me…

She straightened her shoulders and kept walking.

I need you now.
But needing did no good.

GRANT'S HANDS CLENCHED into fists as he watched Scarlett Stone walk away. *I love you.* She'd never told him that before, but he'd known…he'd known how she felt. With Scarlett, there were never any games. No pretending. Her emotions shone in her deep, warm chocolate eyes.

So he'd known exactly how much he was hurting her as he'd told her that he was leaving.

Grant took a step forward, almost called out to her.

But…

He couldn't tell her where he was going. What he was doing. The next mission was black ops. The mission he'd been fighting to take. He loved the adrenaline. He loved the rush. He loved protecting his country and doing his damn best to make the world a better place.

He also…

"I love you, Scarlett," he whispered. But she didn't hear him.

Scarlett was already gone.

Funny…he hadn't realized how cold the summer night felt. Not until that moment.

Chapter One

Ten years later...

His building should have been empty. It was after 7:00 p.m. and McGuire Securities *should* have been shut down for the night.

Grant McGuire was heading out of the place, more than ready to go meet his brothers at a local bar in Austin, Texas. It had been one hell of a week, and he needed to let off some steam.

So when he opened his office door and stepped into the lobby, he thought the place would be deserted.

It wasn't.

A woman was there. She stood just two feet away, as if she'd just entered the lobby and had been making her way directly to see *him*. Her blond hair was pulled away from her face, secured in a little twist at her nape. Her eyes—dark, wide, deep—flared when she saw him.

And the world seemed to stop for Grant.

Scarlett? Scarlett Stone?

Without speaking, he drank her in. His gaze swept over her face. The soft curve of her cheeks, the delicate jaw, the light sprinkling of freckles across her nose. Scarlett had always hated those freckles, but he'd loved them. Had wanted to kiss every single—

"Grant? Um, do you…do you remember me?" Her voice was halting.

As if he could ever forget her. The woman starred in pretty much every fantasy he'd ever had.

She'd changed over the years. She wasn't wearing dusty jeans and a loose T-shirt like she'd favored back in her high school days. She was dressed in black— expensively cut pants and a close-fitting turtleneck. Her feet were encased in high heels— red heels that made him think of sex.

Sex with Scarlett.

"Uh…" Pink flashed across her cheeks as she seemed to decide that no, he didn't remember her. "I'm Scarlett… Scarlett Stone."

A growl built in his throat. "I damn well know who you are." Had he really just been staring at her like a love sick fool? But…Scarlett shouldn't be here. She should be far away from him. Safely away.

He'd made the sacrifice before. Done the right thing by her. So why was she back? In *his* office?

He glanced over her shoulder, his focus shifting to the McGuire Securities entrance. "How did you get in here?" He'd thought the place was locked up.

"Your assistant met me. She was leaving when I was arriving. She told me that you were still here." Scarlett's hands clenched around the small black bag that she carried. "Can we…can we go inside your office to talk?"

The tremble in her voice pierced right through him. Scarlett's voice had shaken like that before. When she was scared, it was a dead giveaway to her emotions. Grant backed into his office, holding the door open for her. When she passed by him, he caught her scent—vanilla.

Did she know that he couldn't smell vanilla without thinking of her?

No. Don't let her see...

He pulled in a deep breath, took in more of her delectable scent, and made sure his mask was in place. The mask he'd always tried to wear around her.

Ten years... He should have gotten over her by now.

"Have a seat," he told her as he turned on more lights and then shut the door.

Scarlett slowly settled into a chair across from his desk. She looked so polished and perfect. Not like the young girl who'd always had her hair streaming over her shoulders and a smile on her face. A smile for him, anyway. A smile that had lit her dark eyes and made—

"Do you recall what you told me? The last time we were—were together?" She fumbled a bit over those words.

He didn't sit behind the desk. He leaned in front of it, positioning his body a few feet from Scarlett. "I'm afraid you're going to have to be more specific for me." He kept his voice controlled. "It's been ten years." Ten years, and wasn't she supposed to be married? His gaze darted to her left hand. No ring.

But she'd been scheduled to get married two months ago. He knew she had. To a lawyer named Eric Turner.

Grant might not be in Scarlett's life, but he kept tabs on her.

Like that doesn't sound crazy.

But he'd been out of town for the past few weeks working on a case. He'd just gotten back to Austin last night, and he didn't know if he was staring at a married woman...or a single one.

"More specific?" Her fingers were white around that black bag. "Right." She cleared her throat. "Okay, you said that if I ever needed you, you'd be there for me." Her gaze held his, and was full of hope. "Now do you remember?"

He'd always been afraid that her eyes could see into his soul. See straight into the darkness that lurked there. "Yes, I remember." He remembered that he'd always been willing to do anything for her.

Scarlett's breath whispered out. "Good. Because, Grant, I'm going to have to call you on that promise."

He frowned at her.

"I need you," she told him as she wet her lips. "I'm desperate, and without your help...I don't know what's going to happen." She glanced over her shoulder, her nervous stare darting to the door.

"Scarlett?" Her fear was palpable, and it made his muscles tense.

"They'll be coming for me soon. I only have a few minutes, and please, *please* stick to your promise. No matter what they say."

He shot away from his desk, his relaxed pose forgotten as he realized that Scarlett wasn't just afraid. She was terrified. "Who's coming?"

"I didn't do it." She rose, too, and dropped her bag into her chair. "It will look like I did, all the evidence says so...but I didn't do it."

He stepped toward her, touched her and felt the jolt slide all the way through him. Ten years...*ten years*... and it was still there. The awareness. The need.

Did she feel it, too?

Focus. "Slow down," Grant told her, trying to keep his voice level and calm. "Just take it easy. You're safe here." *With me.*

But that wasn't exactly true. She was in the most danger when she was with him. Only Scarlett had never realized that fact.

"Say you'll help me," she pleaded. Her tone was desperate. She had a soft voice, one that was perfect for whispering in the dark. A voice that had tempted a boy... and sure as hell made the man he'd become think sinful thoughts.

"I'll help you," Grant heard himself say instantly. So he still had the same problem—he couldn't deny her anything.

Her shoulders sagged in apparent relief. "You've changed." Then her hand rose. Her fingers skimmed over his jaw, rasping against the five o'clock shadow that roughened his face. They were so close right then. And memories collided between them.

When she'd been eighteen, he'd always been so careful with her. He'd had to maintain his control at every moment. But that control had broken one summer night, weeks after her eighteenth birthday...

I can still feel her around me.

"Grant?"

She wasn't eighteen any longer.

And his control—

He heard voices then, coming from the lobby.

"Keep your promise," Scarlett said.

What the hell?

He pulled away from her and walked toward the door.

Those voices were louder now. Because they were... shouting for Scarlett?

"Scarlett Stone...!"

"They were behind me." Her words rushed out. "I knew they were closing in, but I wanted to get to you."

He hated the fear in her voice. "You're safe."

"No, I'm not." She sounded so certain.

Grant opened his office door. Two men were in the lobby. One wore a suit—expensive, well cut. The other was wearing a faded leather jacket and had a badge clipped to his belt.

Why is a cop looking for Scarlett? And it wasn't just any cop. Grant recognized Shayne Townsend because he and the detective had worked a few cases in the past.

"What's happening here?" Grant demanded.

The guy in the suit narrowed his eyes on him. "Who are you?"

Grant's brows rose. He sure didn't like that arrogant, demanding tone. "Grant McGuire. This is *my* business you're in."

Shayne looked over Grant's shoulder. His eyes narrowed and Grant knew he had spied Scarlett. "Ms. Stone," the detective murmured, his face determined. "You need to come with us."

Us? Was the other guy a cop, too? Because Grant didn't recognize him.

But when the suit advanced, Grant braced his legs apart and gave the guy a go-to-hell stare. "She doesn't need to go anyplace. But you two…unless you have some sort of reason for being on my property, a warrant—"

"We're here for Scarlett," the suit said. His blue eyes were blazing with fury. "You can't run anymore, Scarlett."

She had been running…

Shayne pulled out a pair of handcuffs. "Scarlett Stone…" His voice was heavy, emotionless. Grant knew the detective tried to never let emotion influence him on the job. "You're under arrest."

"What?" Grant roared.

Scarlett walked past him then, heading right toward the cop. She'd known the officer was hunting her? That Shayne Townsend was tracking her to Grant's office?

A cuff snicked around one delicate wrist.

"Are those necessary?" Grant demanded. Sure, he'd seen plenty of criminals get cuffed, but Scarlett was no criminal. She was…Scarlett.

"You can bet they're necessary!" the suit all but shouted back at him.

The guy was getting on Grant's last nerve.

"You're under arrest for the murder of Eric Turner," Shayne told her, as the other cuff slid into place. "You have the right to remain silent. You have the right to an attorney—"

Grant shook his head. This wasn't happening. "Scarlett?"

"I didn't do it," she said, glancing over at him with tears in her eyes.

"Yes, you did," the suit snarled. "You killed my brother!"

Oh, hell.

Scarlett was still looking at Grant. "I need you," she said.

And he nodded.

I need you, too. When Shayne started to lead her from the lobby, Grant made damn sure he left with them.

SHE COULDN'T STOP SHAKING. Scarlett had been fingerprinted, searched, caged…the nightmare wouldn't end.

She was in a cell, a small nine-by-ten-foot space that smelled of antiseptic and waste. She was afraid to move. Afraid to speak.

Terrified.

Grant has to keep his promise. Right then, he was her only hope.

She'd known that the cops were after her. She'd pulled into her condo's parking lot, seen Detective Shayne Townsend waiting…and she'd panicked. She'd driven away as fast as she could, and gone to the only man who could help her.

If he would help her.

She'd been back in Austin for only about a year. She'd deliberately stayed away from Grant during that time, but she'd known he was in the city. He and his brothers had all come home five years before.

When their parents had been murdered.

And now here I am...in a cell, accused of murder.

He was probably rethinking his promise to help her. Probably getting ready to turn his back on her and just walk away. If he hadn't already.

Her head sagged forward. This couldn't be happening to her. It was a nightmare.

A door opened, metal scraping over the floor. It was the door that led back to the holding area where she was currently secured. She heard footsteps approaching, but Scarlett didn't look up. She didn't want the guards to see her fear.

The fear that was consuming her.

"Did you do it?"

That wasn't a guard's voice. It was *his* voice. Grant's.

Her head shot up even as she surged to her feet and leaped toward the bars. Grant stood on the other side of them, looking grim, dangerous.

Strong.

Same old Grant. Time had sure been kind to him.

"I told you...I didn't." Her fingers curled around the bars. They were cold to the touch. "I'm being set up. I could never kill anyone!"

"I talked to Detective Townsend. Shayne and I...we know each other..."

Because Shayne Townsend had worked on the murder

case involving Grant's parents? Oh, this was not going well at all.

"Your fingerprints were on the knife that killed the victim, Scarlett."

"Because I'd used the knife before. Used it for making a meal…not to kill Eric. I would never do something like that. Never!"

Grant's jaw locked. "You were seen arguing with your…your fiancé."

Her hold tightened on the bars. "He wasn't my fiancé anymore. That's why we were arguing." She shook her head. "I know it looks bad—"

"His blood was on your clothes!"

She flinched. Grant had definitely had a long talk with the detective. "Because I found him. I thought he might still be alive, and I was trying to save Eric." But he'd already been gone and so cold. Blood had soaked his shirt and pooled beneath him. She closed her eyes, wishing she could shut out that sight, but it was burned into her memory. "I know the evidence is pointing to me, but I didn't do it."

Grant's fingers brushed over hers.

Scarlett's eyes flew open. He had aged so well over the years. The innocence of his youth was gone, replaced by an appearance of rugged power. His face was leaner, but still as handsome. Always handsome… Sculpted lips— lips that some thought held a cruel edge, but she'd always thought his mouth was sexy. Always thought *he* was sexy. A faint scar curved over his square jaw, a silent testimony to the battles he'd fought over the years.

His eyes…that green was harder now, too. He stared out at the world—at her—with suspicion.

The boy she'd loved was gone.

The man who'd taken his place was a stranger.

"I used to be able to tell when you were lying to me." His voice was low, measuring.

Her breath had stilled in her lungs. "I'm not lying," she forced herself to say. *I'm just desperate. So afraid.*

His fingers curled fully around hers as her right hand fisted around the bar. "Why weren't you engaged any longer?"

That was the question he asked her? Her gaze shifted to his throat. She didn't want to look him in the eyes then. She couldn't. "Because I couldn't marry a man I didn't love."

"Scarlett…"

Stare into his eyes. Do it! She lifted her gaze. "You're a private detective now. You have your own agency, and I've—I've read stories about you and your brothers. How successful you are." Not just there in Austin, but all over Texas. Heck, all over the South and up the East Coast. They weren't just some local branch of PIs. They were a force to be reckoned with.

Once upon a time, folks in the area had whispered about the five McGuire boys…boys who'd been wild and reckless. Who'd had a reputation for trouble.

Then those boys had all joined the military.

Grant had been a ranger. Davis and Brodie, the twins, had become SEALs. Mac had been in Delta Force and the youngest brother, Sullivan, had morphed into a marine with a brutal edge.

They'd all been serving their country. They'd been steadfast in their duty. Until their parents had been murdered.

And now I've brought Grant into another murder investigation.

Being involved in her case had to be the last thing he wanted, but he truly was her best chance of survival.

"If anyone can prove that I'm innocent," she added, "it will be you."

She *was* innocent.

"I can pay you," she said, the words tumbling out. "Name a price, I'll pay anything…do anything—"

His head tilted as he studied her. "Yes, you will."

Her heart thundered in her chest. "You'll help me? You won't leave me on my own?"

"I don't break my promises." He towered over her. Grant was easily six foot three, and his body was pure sculpted power. "I gave you my word, and I'll stick to it."

The relief Scarlett felt almost made her dizzy.

"But you will owe me." He backed away, and Scarlett immediately missed his touch. "And I'll be collecting on everything you owe." Grant gave her a nod. Then his gaze swept around the cell and his face hardened. "First order of business will be getting you the hell out of here."

That wasn't happening. At least, not tonight. She wasn't supposed to go before a judge until the next day. Then he might keep holding her… *What if I don't get out at all? All during the trial, locked up.* Scarlett trembled.

"I'm scared." That confession broke from her. She didn't know what strings Grant had pulled to get access to her, but she was just grateful to have him there with her. The years—the distance—had vanished, and she found herself being able to confess to him as easily as she'd shared all her secrets years ago.

At her words, his face hardened even more. "I won't let anyone hurt you."

She leaned closer to the bars, closer to him. "Grant—"

The metal door opened again. "Time's up, McGuire!" a loud voice called.

Grant didn't turn away, not yet. "Trust me," he told her.

She nodded. She'd always trusted Grant.

He backed away.

Her eyes were on him until the heavy metal door swung shut once more. Scarlett kept holding the cold cell bars as she wondered how her life had wound up like this...

You still love him! You think I don't know? You think I'm not aware of what you've been doing, all this time? Eric's voice thundered through her mind. Their last night together. Their last argument.

She'd never expected things to turn so ugly with Eric. Never expected the fight to get so bad. She'd given him back the ring that fateful night. She'd told him she just couldn't marry him.

He'd scared her that night, when she'd always thought he was such a safe guy before.

Maybe Grant would never need to know the full truth about what had happened. Because she had changed a lot in the past ten years. And now...now Grant wouldn't be able to tell when she was lying.

She'd grown too used to lies.

IT WAS HAPPENING. The cops had finally taken in Scarlett Stone. The grand jury had indicted her. There wasn't going to be an escape this time.

She'd pay for what she'd done.

She'd suffer.

This payback...it was such a long time coming. He'd had to plan so carefully to make certain that he struck Scarlett at her weakest point.

Had the woman really believed that she'd get away from him? That she'd find some ridiculous happy ending with another man?

No, Scarlett...that will never happen.

He'd taken away her dreams. Now...now the justice

system would take away her life. He'd be sure to attend all the court proceedings. Watching her suffer would be so rewarding.

You'll suffer, just the way I did.

Scarlett had wrecked his life, and now she was about to see just how much pain she could endure.

She would have nothing. No one.

In the end, he'd be the only one there, laughing as she was taken away—forever.

Chapter Two

The judge had granted bail. The judge had granted bail. But…

It was too high. Scarlett turned to her lawyer, thanking him for what he'd done. "I don't have that much money, Pierce." Pierce Jennings had been the best lawyer she could afford. And he'd done his job—he'd gotten *bail*.

Pierce, perfectly polished as always in his designer suit, patted her hand. "Don't worry." His bright green eyes connected with her stare. "I've been assured the bail is already covered."

What?

The judge was leaving the bench. Scarlett was about to be taken away again. Her gaze darted into the crowded courtroom behind her. Reporters were there. Faces she'd never seen. Eric's brother, Justin, glared at her from his seat behind the prosecutor and—

"Scarlett."

Grant appeared, just a few feet from her, as he pushed through the crowd. When he reached her, his fingers curled over her shoulders. "You'll be out by dusk," he promised her. His eyes glittered. "You'll be with me."

She shook her head. "I don't…I don't have that much

money." Maybe if she mortgaged her condo and sold her car and—

"You'll be with me," he said again, sounding absolutely certain, and she realized that Grant was planning to put up bail for her.

"You can't!" It was too much.

"It's already done." He squeezed her shoulder. She knew the reporters had to be avidly watching this scene. How long would it be before someone dug into her past and found out about her history with Grant?

Not long at all.

"I'll be waiting for you," Grant promised her.

She was about to be led away from him. Reporters were shouting at her. Justin's glare could have melted a glacier, but—

Grant was the only person who mattered to her then. "Thank you," she whispered.

He inclined his head.

THE REPORTERS WERE GONE. The crowd had finally thinned. Grant paced in the narrow hallway, waiting for Scarlett to be released.

She'd been held too long. She'd been too pale. Her eyes too desperate in that courtroom.

"My brother was right…"

Grant swung around at the low, rough voice. Justin Turner stalked toward him. He'd made it a point of learning the guy's identity right away.

The guy's suit was rumpled, his eyes bloodshot. Justin lifted his hand and pointed his shaking finger at Grant. "You were sleeping with his fiancée."

What in the hell?

"He told me that she was involved with someone else.

Even mentioned your name." Justin Turner's laughter was cold. "I told him that he was wrong. Scarlett seemed so good, so perfect. I thought he had to be wrong about her." The man raked a hand through his dark hair. "But he wasn't."

Grant's shoulders tightened. "You don't know what you're talking about."

"Don't I? I watched you in that courtroom. You couldn't take your eyes off her. And the way you touched her..." Disgust flashed over his face.

Grant shook his head. "You're drunk." He could smell the booze wafting off the guy.

"He was my brother! You've got brothers of your own...how would you feel if a woman killed one of them? A woman who claimed to be in love, then turned and attacked—"

The door opened behind Grant. He shifted his body and saw Scarlett standing in the doorway. The light shone off her blond hair, and when she saw Grant, a tentative smile lifted the edges of her full lips.

"Her lover..." Justin snarled. "Eric was right."

Her smile vanished.

Grant took her hand. "Come on, we're leaving." But when he turned back around, Justin was in his path.

"Her last lover was murdered," Justin told Grant. The scent of whiskey clung to the man. After the court appearance, he must have hit the nearest bar—*hard*. "Better not sleep too soundly with her in your bed."

Grant had pulled away from Scarlett and lifted his fist before he even realized—

"Don't!" she yelled. She grabbed his hand. "Please... please, let's just go."

Grant sucked in a deep breath. Holy hell, he *never* lost control like that.

And Justin…he was grinning. The guy had wanted Grant to attack him. Maybe he wasn't as drunk as he appeared.

Grant locked his arm around Scarlett's shoulders. He pulled her up against him. "Get out of our way."

Justin backed off. His eyes were on Scarlett, though, and Grant stiffened at the emotions he saw in the man's eyes. Fury. Hate. So much hate.

"I'm sorry about your brother," Scarlett murmured. "But I didn't do this. I didn't!"

Two guards were watching them, suspicion heavy on their faces.

Scarlett's lawyer was in the hallway, too. Pierce Jennings nervously cleared his throat. "Time to get her out of here," he said to Grant.

It was past time for that. Grant guided Scarlett down the hallway, making sure to keep his hold tight around her. They went out the back exit, just in case any particularly dogged reporters had wanted to try and catch them by surprise.

But no one was out there. Grant opened the passenger-side door of his SUV, and Scarlett slid inside. He hurried around the vehicle.

A glance back showed that Justin had followed them out. The guy stood at the curb, watching them. No, watching Scarlett.

Grant jumped in the car and slammed his door.

"Were you involved with him?" He'd already started digging into Scarlett's life—and so had his brothers. They would soon know every secret that she possessed.

But Grant didn't want to wait for this information. He needed to know right then.

"I was engaged to Eric, you know that—"

"Not Eric. Justin."

"What? No, of course not."

Grant shot out of the parking lot. Left Justin in the dust.

The scent of vanilla drifted to him. Vanilla...still?

"You...you didn't have to pay my bail."

The SUV cut quickly through the streets. A light rain had fallen, and the black pavement gleamed in the growing night.

"Thank you," she said, her voice soft. "I *will* find a way to repay you."

"We already covered that."

He could feel her eyes on him, but Grant kept staring at the road. He wanted to get her back to his place. To have her safe. Then...*then* they'd clear the air.

When did you start to carry so many secrets, Scarlett?

"My brothers are already investigating. This case won't ever go to trial," he said. He just needed to find evidence vindicating her. He *would* find it. Then he'd turn the material over to her lawyer and the DA. They'd get the charges dropped.

"You believe I'm innocent."

She sounded surprised by that.

"You don't even have proof yet—and you believe me?"

"You said you were innocent." He braked at a traffic light, finally looked at her. Damn it, she was so beautiful that she made him ache. He'd never been able to forget her. No matter where he went. Or what he did. He cleared his throat. "You never lied to me."

She glanced away from him, staring out the window. "People can change a lot in ten years."

His head cocked as he studied her. "There's one thing I know…"

Scarlett glanced back at him.

"I know killers." He'd seen plenty during his time— during missions that could never be discussed or forgotten. "And I know that you *aren't* a killer." Knowing and proving, well, those were two very different things.

But I will prove her innocence.

The light changed to green. The vehicle surged forward.

"Where are we going?" Scarlett asked. "My condo is on the other side of town—"

"I know where your condo is." He'd already been there. Already searched through the place. "We're going to my house."

"Your…house?"

He accelerated as they headed toward the outskirts of Austin. He didn't live on his family's ranch, not anymore, but two of his brothers did. "Don't worry we'll have plenty of privacy."

"I wasn't worried about privacy."

"Then what are you worried about?"

Silence.

His jaw locked. "You better get used to the idea of being with me, Scarlett. Because I just put up half a million dollars for your freedom, and until this case is over, you and I will be staying very close to one another."

As close as he could get.

But that wasn't just because of the money.

It was because of…her.

What happens when you realize you made the worst

mistake of your life when you were a clueless, twenty-two-year-old kid?

Answer—you do anything, you do everything, to correct that mistake.

SCARLETT STONE WASN'T in jail any longer. She'd escaped so quickly—with that jerk Grant McGuire at her side.

The McGuires…they'd always thought they were so special. So much better than everyone else.

Wild and reckless as kids, now they thought they were the law in the area?

Hell, *no.*

Grant wasn't getting another chance with Scarlett. Their past was over. Finished.

Just as Grant would be…

One lover in the grave…and another will be joining him.

Scarlett wasn't going to get a happily-ever-after ending. She would only have grief and pain.

SHE WAS IN his house. Grant's house. The place was massive, hidden far from the lights of Austin. No, this wasn't his father's old ranch, but if you headed to the east and kept leaving those bright lights, you'd hit the place.

Too many memories.

The memories were what had kept her away from Austin for so long, and then, eventually, the memories had brought her back.

But Eric thought I came here for him. He got his job transfer, and wanted me to move here with him.

She'd come back to Austin, and the first day after she'd arrived, she'd seen Grant.

He hadn't seen her.

Once, he was the only one who ever seemed to see the real me. Then he'd left.

They were in his den. He was at the bar, pouring a drink. He was going to ask her questions now, and she couldn't lie to him. Not with her life on the line.

"Want a drink?" Grant asked.

"No, thank you."

He laughed as he turned toward her. "Now, Scarlett, aren't we far past the polite stage?"

Her brows climbed. "What stage are we at?" She had no clue.

He brought her a drink. She didn't even know what was in that glass. "The stage where you should trust me," he told her.

She took the glass from him.

"You probably need that," he said, eyes assessing, "after what you've been through."

The past two months had been hell.

Finding Eric's body...the suspicions...then, so recently, the arrest. The cell. *I do need this.*

She drained the contents in a few quick gulps. But the liquid burned and she gasped as tears stung her eyes.

Grant's faint laughter came once more, rolling over her. "I don't think you were made to chug whiskey."

He took her glass and patted her on the back.

She stopped choking.

He didn't stop touching her. She was far too conscious of his touch. The heat from his hand seemed to penetrate right through her clothing.

"I think you were made for other things," he murmured.

Her gaze was caught and held by his. Grant stood so close that his mouth was just inches away. It might be wrong, but she'd never forgotten his kiss.

He'd been the first boy to kiss her. The first to touch her...

The first to break her heart.

Scarlett stepped away from him. "What do you need to know?"

He blinked at her. Then a mask seemed to slide over his face. He lifted his glass and drained his whiskey, but didn't have the choking, gasping issue that she'd had. Of course not.

Scarlett huffed out a breath and paced around the den. There weren't many personal touches in that place. A TV. Two couches. She headed toward the mantel. One framed photograph rested there—a shot of Grant, his siblings and his parents.

They'd been good to me. Grant's parents had been so kind to her after Grant left. After she'd gone to them, they'd wanted to help her...

"I'm sorry about your parents." She said this without looking back at him. "I...came to the funeral, but I didn't want to bother you, so I just—"

"Stayed in the back, behind the oak trees."

She turned toward him in surprise.

"I saw you," he said, inclining his head toward her. "You're a hard woman to miss."

He'd been so stoic at that graveside. He'd stood apart from his siblings. She'd wanted to go to him, to wrap her arms around him and try to comfort him. As a friend.

But...they didn't even have friendship between them, not anymore.

"It's because of your parents, isn't it?" Scarlett murmured as she rubbed at the tension that had knotted the base of her neck. "Their death brought you back."

Back from his missions. From the life that she didn't know anything about.

But…

He carried a scar now. Small, thin, white, the wound marked the skin under the curve of his jaw. But he was damaged by more than just that scar. When she gazed in his eyes, she could see the new shadows that he carried. The new secrets.

"Ava was seventeen when they died," he said, voice low. "She needed us. She…took their death hard."

Ava was his baby sister. A surprise that had come to their family. "She was there, wasn't she?" That was the story Scarlett had read. Ava had been at the ranch house when intruders came in and shot her parents. She'd been there, but she'd escaped.

"She was there." Grant's voice was grim. "And she still blames herself. She thinks that she could have saved them." He raked a hand through his hair. "If she'd tried, she would have died, too."

Scarlett found herself creeping toward him. Then, because she couldn't stop herself, she wrapped her arms around him. He was stiff and still in her embrace. "I'm sorry. They were good people."

He didn't hug her back, and she began to feel foolish. Hugging him had been an impulse, and obviously, the wrong one to follow. She started to retreat.

Then his arms rose. He curled them around her and held her tightly against him.

And it was like coming home. Being in his arms felt right—when it was wrong. All wrong. The past was over. She'd come to terms with that a long time ago.

"You still smell like vanilla."

His voice was a growl. His body was so warm and hard.

"Every time I smell vanilla, I think of you." His voice was a rumble that seemed to vibrate right through her whole body.

She tried to pull away then. Nothing good would come from getting in too deep with Grant. She had to protect herself. She was already in enough trouble as it was.

But he wasn't letting her go.

Her head tilted back. She stared up at him.

"No other woman has eyes like you do." His voice was still that low, sensual rumble. "So dark and deep. And every time those eyes lock on me, I wonder…*how deep does she see into me?*"

"Grant…"

His gaze fell to her mouth. "I always liked the way you said my name."

His head was lowering toward hers. Despite everything, Scarlett wanted him to kiss her, because it had been far too long since she'd felt his lips against her own.

But she was terrified. He *couldn't* kiss her. She wouldn't, couldn't repeat the same mistakes from her past. And getting personally involved with Grant McGuire would be a huge mistake.

Because Grant *couldn't* love her. He never had, and he never would.

"Let me go," she whispered, even though just an inch separated their mouths.

"What if I don't want to?" He surrounded her. "Don't you want to see if it's as good between us now…as it was then? Because I do."

It would be as good. Their chemistry had always been electric. Her body yearned for him.

Mistake. Mistake. She'd been charged with murdering her ex-fiancé. She'd barely been released on bail. She couldn't do this.

"Let me go," Scarlett said again.

Surprisingly, he did.

She backed away from him, a few quick, desperate steps. Scarlett sucked in fast gulps of air.

Grant watched her. "You still want me."

Desire faded with time. It had to fade. Ten years should have killed it, but...

It didn't.

"And, just so we're clear," Grant continued, as his pupils expanded to swallow the green of his gaze, "I can't look at you without wanting you naked and in my bed."

She lost the breath she'd taken.

"Just so we're clear," he murmured again.

They were more than clear. Her heart was racing. Her body aching. "We...can't."

"I think we can." His head tilted as he studied her. His gaze, burning with desire, swept over her. "I think we will."

She could only shake her head. "Don't you wonder? I mean, even a little bit..."

He waited.

"How can you be so sure I'm not dangerous? That I'm not a threat to you?"

He started stalking toward her. Instinctively, Scarlett backed up. She retreated until her shoulders hit the bricks that lined his fireplace.

"Baby, do I look like I'm afraid?"

He'd never looked afraid—of anything or anyone. But he was also very, very different from the boy she'd known. "What happened to you?" Scarlett asked him softly.

"War. Death." His voice was grim. "So trust me when I say that I can handle any threat that comes my way."

She swallowed. She felt trapped, more caged than she had when she'd been back in her prison cell.

And he wasn't even touching her.

"Grant...I need us to keep the past—"

His eyelids flickered.

"In the past," she finished softly. "Too much is on the line. I have to find out who killed Eric. *Why* he was killed."

Grant's jaw hardened. "I will find out. I'll clear you."

And then she'd owe him. That knowledge was there, pushing between them.

He sighed softly then took a step back. "I need to know about your fiancé's enemies."

He wasn't my fiancé. Not at the end.

"Eric...he was a tax attorney. He got along great with his clients." She rubbed her chilled arms. "He didn't have enemies." He'd been a likable guy. Making friends everywhere he went. *Pierce Jennings is my lawyer because he knew Eric, too. We'd met at a party. Everyone loved Eric.*

Everyone...but her. No matter how hard she'd tried to love him.

Grant shook his head. "We all have enemies." He paced away from her. "And the nature of his death... Knife attacks are more personal. Intimate. There were no signs of a break-in at his place, so the guy might have even let his attacker inside. It was someone he trusted. Someone—"

"Like me." That was certainly what the cops thought.

Grant stopped pacing and faced her fully. "You know my brothers and I will have to uncover every secret that you have."

She was well aware of that. She also hated for him to dig too deeply into her past.

"So if there's something you need to tell me, then do it now."

Scarlett licked her lips. "There's nothing that relates to this case."

"Scarlett…"

"*Nothing* that relates." She lifted her chin. "I don't know anyone who would want to hurt Eric. He was a nice guy. A good person."

She should have been able to love him.

"I never even saw him get angry. Not until that last night." When she'd told him that she couldn't marry him. *All this time…you've made me wait. You kept me dangling on a damn string—and you think I'm just going to let you go now?*

She hated those memories. The last time she'd seen Eric…it had been so rough for them both. "I hurt him," she whispered.

Grant's eyes narrowed.

"He only wanted to love me, to make me happy." She pushed back her hair. "I moved back to Austin when he got his job transfer, and he thought we were going to get married. Going to…have kids."

Grant's eyes were tight slits.

"He waited for me. Kept letting me push back the wedding date. He was a *good man*," she said again. "And he didn't deserve what happened to him. He didn't deserve *anything* that happened."

She didn't just want to prove her own innocence. "I want to find the man who did this to him. I want to give Eric justice." It was the only thing she could give him. "The same way you're hunting for your parents' killer. I want justice, too."

He gave her a smile. Cold, slightly cruel. *I don't know him any longer.* Because that was a stranger staring back at her. "Who says I want justice? I'm looking for vengeance, and one day, I'll have it."

Goose bumps rose on her arms and she trembled.

Grant glanced away from her. His eyes slid toward the darkened hallway. "You're exhausted. Take the first room on the right. We can talk in the morning."

She wanted to run to that room and escape. She hadn't been able to sleep at all in her cell. Every sound had terrified her.

He was between her and the hallway. Scarlett squared her shoulders and headed toward him.

He didn't back away as she approached. Tension made her steps hurried.

"Even good men can carry dark secrets."

His words had her stumbling.

"It's not just your life I have to rip apart. It's his, too. I hope you're prepared for what I might find."

"I'm not prepared for any of this." She gave Grant a brittle smile. "But that doesn't matter, does it?" She was trapped in this hell, and she had to survive. One way or another.

She put one foot in front of the other and reached the hallway. Her fingers rose and pressed against the wall. "I never imagined it would be this way." She spoke without looking back at him. "When I thought about…us… Seeing you again… I never thought I'd be so desperate."

There was silence, then he asked, "What did you think it would be like?"

For an instant, she almost smiled. A real smile. "You were supposed to have put on about two hundred pounds. You were supposed to be bald and you were supposed to desperately yearn for me. You were supposed to wish that you'd never left me behind." Now she did look back at him.

His expression was inscrutable.

"You weren't supposed to be my only hope. You *weren't* supposed to be the man I had to beg."

He gave a hard shake of his head. "You never have to beg me for anything."

She did. For her survival, and it made her feel ashamed. Weak.

"Good night, Grant." She stepped into the hallway.

"This isn't the way I thought it would be, either."

She wouldn't let his words stop her.

"You weren't supposed to be even more beautiful. You weren't supposed to still make me ache…*and you weren't supposed to be with another man.*"

She wasn't with anyone else. Not any longer.

"You were supposed to be with me."

His words made her stumble again. She rushed into the room on the right. Shut the door.

Sagged against the wood.

You were supposed to be with me. Those words had pierced straight to her heart. The heart he'd claimed, long ago.

The heart he'd tossed away.

I will be stronger this time. I won't make the same mistakes.

She glanced around the room. Realized she was in *his* bedroom. Scarlett started to walk right back out of that room, but…

But the bed looked too inviting.

And I'm finally safe.

Because if there was one thing she *could* count on, it was that Grant would protect her. She never doubted her ex-ranger on that score.

But who will protect me from him?

Her fingers slid over the lock on the door. She turned it and the distinctive click filled the air.

I'll protect myself.

Because she knew that she couldn't survive another Grant McGuire heartbreak. And she *wouldn't* give him the chance to hurt her again.

JUSTIN TURNER STARED at the dark house. The lights had been on moments before, but then the place had plunged into darkness.

Scarlett was in that house. With Grant McGuire.

He knew all about McGuire. Most of Austin had heard of the man. Dangerous, determined…Grant McGuire's reputation preceded him.

The guy had opened his PI business a few years back. And he'd been working to help victims since then.

Scarlett isn't a victim. She was a killer. Grant should see her for exactly what she was.

But Justin hadn't been able to see the truth, either. Not at first. Like his brother, he'd been blinded by her beauty. By her dark eyes and her high-voltage smile. He'd been blind, and now Eric was *dead*.

Scarlett wasn't going to get away with murder. Justin would make absolutely sure of it.

I can't wait for you to meet Scarlett… His brother's voice, jovial and light, ran back through his mind. *I know you'll love her just as much as I do.*

No, he didn't.

His eyes stayed on that darkened house.

Chapter Three

The pounding at his front door woke Grant the next morning. A quick glance at the nearby clock told him it was barely 6:00 a.m. Way too early for any normal visitor. He jumped out of the guest bed, dragged on a pair of jeans and headed down the hallway.

Scarlett opened her door just as he was passing her. She was wearing one of his old army shirts—he'd forgotten to bring her clothes over—and looking so sexy that he came to a dead stop.

"What's happening?" she asked, her voice soft. "I… is someone here?"

That pounding came again. Yes, some bozo was there. Too early. Grant pulled his gaze off the long expanse of her legs and finished making his way to the front door. A quick glance out the peephole revealed that he wasn't being harassed by some too aggressive, jerk reporter.

It was just his brother.

Who could be quite a jerk in his own right.

Grant pulled open the door. Sullivan, his youngest brother, stood on the threshold, glowering. That was hardly surprising. Sullivan always wore that hard, angry expression.

He'd worn it since they'd buried their parents, five years before.

"You aren't supposed to be here," Grant told him. "You had a case you were working in New York—"

"Finished it last night." Sullivan pushed by him. He was close to Grant's own six foot three height. But while Grant had light hair, Sullivan's was as dark as night. His eyes—eyes the same shade of green as Grant's own—glittered. "And on the way back, I *finally* heard about the mess you got tangled in." He gave a low whistle. "Man, what were you thinking? To get involved with *her* again? Especially after she killed someone!"

"Ah, Sullivan…"

"I get it." His brother waved away the interruption. "She's hot. Always was smokin'."

Grant's eyes narrowed. Sullivan and Scarlett had been in the same class. He just hadn't realized that his little brother had been quite so…aware of her.

"And you've always had a crazy weakness for her."

Grant could feel his cheeks burning. *"Sullivan."*

"But she's trouble. I read press reports about this case. That's all I *could* read on the flight back. She killed one lover, and you're going to whisk her right out of that courtroom without even—"

"I didn't kill him." Scarlett's voice wasn't so soft anymore. It was angry. Fierce.

Sullivan's face went slack with shock. *"You've got her in your house already?"*

Not just his house, his bed.

Sullivan turned to face Scarlett.

Smokin'…yes, with her hair rumpled and her legs bare, she was definitely a sight to behold. Red stained her cheeks and her eyes shone with a dark fire.

"I didn't kill my lover, Sullivan. The stories in the papers and online are all wrong." Her lips tightened. "And so are you."

Sullivan rocked back on his heels. "She's wearing your shirt."

She was.

"Think with your head, bro!" Sullivan's glare fired at Grant. "This woman wrecked you once—"

Grant grabbed his brother by the shirtfront and shoved him against the nearest wall. "Not another word." It was a lethal whisper.

Sullivan blinked at him.

"She's innocent," he growled.

Sullivan shook his head.

"I know Scarlett. She wouldn't take a knife and shove it into a man's chest again and again." That wasn't her. Scarlett was no monster. To him, she was one of the few good things in the world.

He'd needed to remember her when he'd been in one hell after another. *A good thing...in a world gone bad.*

"You don't know her..." Sullivan gritted his teeth in turn, his jaw locking. "You haven't seen her in ten years."

He had seen her. Sometimes, he'd needed to see her in order to get through the darkness that wanted to consume him.

"Uh..." Scarlett's footsteps padded closer and then she tapped Grant on his shoulder. "I get that the McGuire brothers have always liked to play rough and all, but I think you should let your brother go."

A faint smile curved Sullivan's lips.

Jerk. But Grant released him.

Sullivan took his time straightening his T-shirt, as if Grant had done some kind of damage. Sullivan was an ex-marine. The guy could handle a hard shove—or twenty.

If he reveals too much to Scarlett, I'll give him plenty of damage to handle.

"I didn't kill Eric," Scarlett said, her words rushing

out. "And I'm here…because Grant is going to help me find the person who did."

Sullivan raised his brows at that.

"Davis and Brodie are already working the case," Grant told him, referring to their twin brothers. "I didn't call you in because I knew you were close to wrapping things up in New York. We were handling this…"

Sullivan's gaze dipped over Scarlett's body. "I'm sure you were handling plenty."

Grant started to lunge forward.

But Scarlett was still touching him. Her fingers tightened around his shoulder. "It's not like your brother is the only one who thinks I'm guilty. The grand jury indicted me. The press is flaying me and plenty of people feel the same way." Her hand dropped. "That's why we have to find the killer."

Before she could back away, Grant caught her hand. Soft, delicate. It hardly looked like the hand that would curl around a knife and viciously stab a man to death. His fingers smoothed over hers. He wondered when she'd stopped wearing Eric's ring. There was a faint tan line on her left ring finger and he wanted to ask her—

Grant swore. "You're left-handed." He remembered that now. When they'd been dating, he'd teased her a few times about being a leftie when they played a bit of baseball together.

"Uh, yes, I am."

His head snapped up. His gaze pinned Sullivan. He hadn't been planning to call in Sullivan, but since his brother was there… "We need to go over the ME's reports. See if the attack is consistent with a left-handed or right-handed perp." Because the results would be different. The angle of attack, the thrust of the blade—all different for a left-handed person. "We have to go over that report, immediately!" They might even need to get their own expert to review the injuries. Excitement thickened Grant's voice. This was just one piece of the puzzle, and it could be a long shot, but…

It's a starting point. If the killer wasn't left-handed, then that's one piece of evidence pointing to Scarlett's innocence.

Sullivan's eyes widened. "You're doing this for her."

"No, *we* are." Because the McGuires worked together. "We hunt for killers. We protect the—"

"She's no killer, and we're going to prove it."

Their parents' murders had hit Sullivan so hard. He'd stopped trusting people and started to look at everyone outside his family with too much suspicion.

Grant glanced back at Scarlett. "We need to visit that crime scene today. I want you to walk me through every single moment…from the instant you stepped through that door until the cops arrived." Because maybe there was something there. Some small piece of evidence that had been overlooked by the police.

Such as Scarlett being left-handed.

Eventually, the small pieces would add up, and they'd unmask the real killer.

Hope lit Scarlett's eyes, and it was a beautiful thing. He stared at her, lost for a minute. Once, she'd always looked out at the world with hope.

Then he'd met her one summer evening, and he'd watched hope—hope for their future—fade from her eyes.

"I'll get dressed." She threw her arms around Grant. "Thank you."

He wanted to hold her tight, but didn't. He didn't hold her at all. Then she let him go.

He couldn't take his eyes off her as she hurried away from him.

When she disappeared down the hallway, Sullivan spoke, his voice low. "This is a mistake. I'm going on record as saying so."

"I told you already that she didn't do it."

"Right...because you were in the room with her and her lover. You *saw* that she was innocent."

Grant glared at his little brother. Marine or no, he'd still be able to take him down any day of the week. "I'm not like you, Sullivan. I didn't stop believing in everyone."

Sullivan shook his head. "And you're also trying to cling to the past. You can't do that. The past is dead." He stalked toward the front door. "And people change, bro. That's a lesson *you* need to learn. She was your angel once, I get that. But you have no idea who—or what— she is now." He yanked open the door. "Watch your back. You don't want to wind up like Eric Turner."

ERIC'S CONDO FELT ice-cold. Scarlett rubbed her arms as she walked inside. She hadn't been in Eric's place...not since the morning she'd found him.

There was still blood staining the hardwood floor. *His* blood.

The door shut behind her. "How'd you get in that morning?" Grant asked her.

Sunlight streamed through the picture window. They'd been arguing, right there...

You think you can leave me now? After everything?

"The door was unlocked. I mean, I had a key, but I didn't have to use it, because when I got here the front door was open." Eric had always kept the door locked, so she'd been worried when she saw it slightly ajar.

"You had a key." Grant paused. "You lived here?"

She shook her head, caught by the hard edge in his voice. "No, Eric wanted me to but…but I had my own place, close to the school." Because she was a teacher, or she had been. Scarlett had already been notified of her suspension from that position. But if she could prove her innocence, she'd get the job back. She'd get her life back.

"Why did you come here that morning?"

"We'd fought the night before, and I didn't like the way we'd left things. So I came over to talk with him again. I wanted to speak with him before I went in to school."

Grant paced into the room and stopped in front of the picture window. No other buildings blocked the perfect view from that window. Scarlett had stood there plenty of times and stared below at the park and then out at the bustling traffic on the streets.

"What did you argue about?" Grant asked.

"The engagement. I gave him back his ring."

Grant turned to face her. "He didn't take it well."

"He had plans, dreams for us." She shook her head, sad as she remembered. "So he was angry."

"Did he get…physical with you?"

She rolled back her shoulders. "Not Eric. Never Eric. He wasn't like that."

Grant frowned, and she realized that her words had revealed a little too much. Scarlett crept forward, feeling like an intruder in Eric's place. "I called out to him, but he didn't answer."

Everything in the condo was just as Eric had left it. His will had been in probate, so maybe Justin hadn't wanted to touch any of his brother's possessions until the will was clear. But with all of Eric's belongings still there, Scarlett almost expected to see him walking toward her.

I'm sorry, Eric.

She could feel him in that place. There had been so much blood on him. On the floor…

She pointed to the stained wood. "A vase of broken flowers was beside him." He'd had that vase prepared for her when she'd arrived the night before. "The knife was to his right. I'd used that knife to make dinner the evening before." And that evening had been a nightmare. She'd realized then, as panic closed in, that she couldn't stay with him. He'd started talking about children, and she'd remembered—

No. Don't go there. Do not.

"That's why my prints were on the knife. I didn't touch it that morning. I fell to my knees beside him. I tried to help him, but it was too late." His blood had soaked her fingers. Her clothes.

Grant stared down at the floor. Then he drew back and started walking around the room. He picked up photographs. A picture of Eric and his brother. One of her and Eric. "How long were you with him?"

"A year and a half." They'd met in Dallas. She'd thought maybe he could be the one for her. *You can't make someone love you…and you can't make yourself love someone.*

Grant put the photo back down. "You think you knew all his secrets?"

Scarlett shook her head. "I don't think he had any secrets."

"We all have them." Grant disappeared into the bedroom.

Scarlett didn't follow him. Her stomach was twisting into knots. He had gotten them into the building, slipping past the line of police tape to get inside the condo, and being in that place was like facing a nightmare.

"The cops searched this place thoroughly," Scarlett

called out. "They didn't find anything that pointed to any suspect…but me."

He was back. Striding toward her with his gloved fingers curled around something. He lifted his hand, and she saw a—business card?

"Maybe they didn't look hard enough. Or maybe they didn't know what to look for."

She took the card from him. "Louis East…private investigator?" Scarlett frowned. "He told me that he hired a PI for a few of his cases, so that's probably—"

"Your name is written on the back of the card."

"What?" She turned it over and recognized Eric's sloping handwriting.

"I told you, we all have our secrets." Grant's fingers curled around the card once more. "I know Louis. The guy tends to have one specialty."

"And what specialty is that?"

"He catches cheating spouses."

Her heart slammed into her chest. "I wasn't cheating on Eric!"

Grant tucked the card into his pocket. Wait, could he just…take that? From Eric's place?

Then he started searching the rest of the condo. No wonder he'd put on gloves before he came inside. He opened cabinet doors, poked into Eric's desk. Eric's laptop was gone, and Scarlett had no idea where it was or—

"None of your things are here." Grant's shoulders were stiff. "Not so much as a hairbrush or a toothbrush."

"I told you, I didn't live here."

He glanced over at her. "But you were sleeping with him."

Her cheeks flamed. "That's personal!" And so not Grant's business at all.

"You don't get to have personal," he growled. "Not when you're facing a life sentence for murder."

She glanced away from him.

"We're done here," he said flatly. "Let's go."

She couldn't wait to get out. Scarlett hurried toward the door. She pulled it open.

And found Justin waiting in the hallway.

The breath left her in a startled rush.

"Came back to the scene of the crime, did you?" Justin muttered, his eyes angry slits. His lips twisted into a furious snarl. *"Back to my brother's home!"*

In the face of his fury, she staggered back. But she didn't have to retreat far. Grant was there. Pulling her behind him. Facing off against Justin.

"You shouldn't be here!" Justin snapped as he ducked under the police tape. "McGuire, you think because you've got half the Austin cops in your back pocket that you can bust into my brother's home?"

"I'm looking for his killer." Grant's voice was flat.

"She's right behind you! You don't have to look hard!"

The rage in his voice scared her. Justin had been unraveling ever since his brother's death. And all his fury was directed at her. *Because he thinks I'm guilty.*

"You can help us." Grant's own voice was calm. "Tell us the names of any enemies your brother had. Tell us—"

Justin's laughter cut him off. "You aren't going to pin this on someone else." He shoved past Grant and his gaze raked Scarlett. "I'm going to be there at the trial. Every day. I will make *certain* that you pay for what you've done."

His voice was raised. He was nearly shouting at her and she wondered if any neighbors would hear him.

No one had heard anything when Eric died.

"Another fool..." Justin's stare was fixed on Grant.

"Eric talked about you, McGuire. He was right, huh? You were with her. All this time." His hands were fists at his sides. "Were you in on it? Did you help her to kill my brother?" Then with a shout, as if he'd been pushed too far by his own fury, Justin attacked. He came at Grant, swinging his trembling fists.

Scarlett didn't even have a chance to scream.

Grant stepped back and dodged one blow. He caught the second fist that Justin sent his way. "You're drunk," Grant said. "Again."

Justin tried to head butt him, but Grant just shoved him back. He hit the nearest wall and his legs seemed to crumple beneath him as Justin sank to the floor.

"Sober up," Grant ordered him with a hard glare. "Then maybe you can see that more is going on here than meets the eye. I didn't kill your brother. Neither did she. But we will find out who did." He reached for Scarlett's hand. "Come on."

Justin didn't get up. He just watched them with bloodshot eyes. "He knew…all along, he knew she was with someone else!"

I wasn't.

"Watching her, following her…*he knew*!"

They ducked under the yellow police tape and slipped back into the hallway. Grant pulled her toward the elevator. She didn't breathe again until those elevator doors slid closed.

Then she realized that Grant still had her wrist in an unbreakable grip. His muscles were tight, his jaw locked. "Was there someone else?"

She shook her head.

"A jealous lover could have killed Eric. *Tell me.* Before Louis East does."

"There's nothing to tell." Her breath whispered out.

"Nothing." Because she'd had a grand total of three lovers in her life.

One of those lovers stood before her.

Another was dead.

And the third...*long gone.*

"Justin is following you."

She shivered. The man's fury scared her.

Grant's eyes raked over her face. "He's not going to hurt you."

If Grant hadn't been there...if she'd been the only one in that condo, looking for clues... "I'm not so sure of that." She hesitated, then said, "Justin has been battling an alcohol problem for a while. Eric told me about it. He was trying to get his brother help—"

Grant swore. "And you didn't think this was important to mention to the police? To me? Eric would have opened his condo door to his brother. He would have let him right inside! And if the guy gets mean when he drinks..."

He did.

"I told the police. They said he had an alibi." She swallowed. The elevator had stopped. "I didn't." She had also been the one covered in blood.

She started to step out into the lobby.

Grant tugged her to a stop. He still held her wrist. "Last chance," he murmured. "You think I can't feel your secrets? Because I can. It's like they're standing right between us."

Tears stung her eyes. *There is no need for him to know. The PI couldn't have found out.*

She shook her head.

"Have it your way." Grant dropped her hand.

And she nearly ran out of the elevator.

I don't ever want to go back to Eric's condo. The image of the bloodstained floors filled her mind, and when she hurried out of the building, even the bright sunlight couldn't banish her chill.

GRANT DIDN'T BOTHER knocking at Louis East's place. He just grabbed the doorknob and shoved open the door to the small office on the rougher side of Austin. The PI was in there, and Louis jumped to his feet with an outraged bellow.

"Hey, who the hell are—*McGuire*."

Scarlett crept in behind Grant. He didn't look back at her.

Louis did. His eyes widened in recognition when he saw her, then narrowed in calculation. "Well, well, isn't this an interesting little party." He sat back down at his desk and waved his hand toward the chairs across from him. "Sorry my assistant wasn't out there to greet you, but—"

"Cut the bull," Grant ordered. He didn't sit. "You don't have an assistant." He stalked forward and slapped his hands on the worn desk. "Why did Eric Turner hire you?"

Once more, Louis's eyes—light blue—darted toward Scarlett. "The usual reason folks hire me," he muttered.

"He thought she was cheating?" Grant had asked Scarlett about another lover even as jealousy had twisted through him. She'd denied it, but...

Louis laughed. "Why are you acting surprised? Though I have to give you both credit, no matter how many times I tailed Scarlett, I could never catch you two together."

You two. Grant straightened. "Eric thought I was her lover?"

Scarlett was silent behind him.

Louis blinked. "Sure…he was certain of it. Said that she was still hung up on you, and he wanted proof of her infidelity." The PI rubbed his hand over his jaw. "Seems some guy told him you were both meeting up, but that Eric…he was hoping the fellow was wrong. Optimistic type, you know? So he hired me."

Grant forced his jaw to unclench. "What guy told him? I need a name."

Louis shrugged. "Don't know a name. He didn't tell me one." His eyes darted toward Scarlett once more. Nervously this time.

Wait…that was more than just a nervous glance. Guilt showed in the man's eyes, for just an instant. The flash appeared then was quickly controlled.

"You never saw us together," Scarlett said as she stalked toward the PI's desk. "Because we *weren't* together."

"Yeah, well, then you probably shouldn't have called Grant here's name at the, uh, wrong time."

Grant heard her shocked inhalation.

He was pretty damn shocked, too.

But Grant didn't look at her. Not yet. *Focus.* "You said you followed her. How long?"

Louis glanced toward his narrow window.

"How long?"

"For a month. Right up until the poor fool's death. Figured there wasn't any point in following her anymore, 'cause no one was around to pay me."

So the guy had cut his losses. Moved on to fresh prey. But something nagged at Grant. "Were you following her the morning she found the body?"

He saw the faint flicker in Louis's eyes.

"You SOB. You were following her! And you didn't tell the cops!" He wanted to rip the guy apart right then.

Louis shot out of his chair and staggered back a step. "I didn't realize what was happening at first. She went in, then ten minutes later the cops roared up. The cops and me...we don't exactly get along so well. Got some conflicts of interest happening, know what I mean?"

"You left," Scarlett whispered.

Louis shrugged once more.

"You could have told them..." She marched behind the desk to close in on Louis. "You could have told them that I was only inside a few minutes! That I didn't have time to kill Eric—"

He wasn't looking her in the eye. "How do I know what you had time to do?"

"The ME said he'd been dead for two hours! You would have *proved* that I couldn't possibly have killed him, if you'd just talked to the cops. You would have confirmed I wasn't there at the time of his death." She grabbed the man's shirt. Shook him. "They arrested me! Tossed me in jail! My life...my life is being shredded in today's paper, and all along *you knew I didn't do it*!"

Grant choked back his own fury. He caught Scarlett's shoulders in his hands and pulled her away from Louis. "You were waiting, right, Louis?" That twisted, money-grubbing weasel. "Waiting until you thought she was good and desperate, and then what? You were going to appear with some evidence for her to use in court? Evidence she could buy? Photos of her entering the condo, with a nice neat time stamp on them?"

The faint flicker of Louis's eyelashes came again and Grant knew he was right on target.

Scarlett tried to lunge for the man again. Grant held her back. "We're calling the cops right now, Louis," he snarled. "We're calling Detective Shayne Townsend. And you're going to tell him everything. You're going to give him those photos, do you understand?"

Louis stared over Grant's shoulder. "What photos?"

"If you try to hold back on this, I will *destroy* you," Grant promised him with lethal intensity. "Trust me, you don't want to tangle with me." He wasn't a pawn for this jerk to play with. And neither was Scarlett.

Louis swiped his hand over his sweaty forehead.

"You can prove I'm innocent," Scarlett whispered. "You can *prove it*!"

Grant yanked out his phone. He dialed the number he'd memorized long ago, then waited. Scarlett was trembling beside him. The phone rang once. Twice—

"Detective Townsend."

"Shayne, it's Grant McGuire. I need you to meet me at East Private Investigations, now."

"Uh, yeah, I'm in the middle of a case—"

"Louis East can prove that Scarlett Stone didn't kill her fiancé. *Ex*-fiancé. "He's got photos. He was *there*."

"What?" Shock made the word crack. "I'm on my way."

Yeah, he'd thought that would be the detective's response. Grant shoved the phone back into his pocket.

He glared at the man who'd let Scarlett suffer. If he hadn't found that card, Louis would have kept silent for months, until he'd gotten a big payoff. Because money was more important to the sleazeball than a woman's life.

"Sit back down," Grant snarled.

Louis glared, but sat back in his chair.

And Scarlett paced away from them, nervous energy seeming to roll off her.

It's going to be all right. You'll be safe. This will be over soon.

"If they read my files, they'll find out everything," Louis said.

Scarlett whirled toward him.

Grant caught the flash of fear on her face.

"You want them learning everything?" Louis pressed. He smiled. His slick, I'm-still-in-the-game smile. "Maybe we can still work something out here, huh?"

Scarlett glanced at Grant. There was definitely fear in her gaze.

"Well, well…" Louis's chair squeaked. "He doesn't know, does he?"

Grant took up a position by the doorway. He wasn't leaving that office, not until Shayne arrived. He wasn't going to risk giving Louis the chance to flee—or to destroy any photos.

"I told Eric. I mean, I had to give the guy something, right? He was footing my bill and he needed results. So I told him…the day before he died."

Grant's eyes narrowed. "What did you tell Eric?"

But Louis was watching Scarlett. "Then I heard that you spread the word you'd broken up with him. You told the cops that spiel, right? *You* broke up with *him*. But that's not really what happened before he died, is it? That guy dumped *you*."

"Stop," Scarlett whispered.

"Because he found out about you and McGuire here…"

"There was nothing to find out," Grant said for what had to be the fourth time. He'd tried to keep his distance from Scarlett. "I stayed away from her."

Louis smiled. "He never knew, did he, Scarlett?"

"Stop," she said again.

"Or at least, you *think* he didn't." Now Louis was looking satisfied, as a smirk twisted his thin lips. "Maybe I can clear you, sweet thing, but what about your lover here? When I talk to the cops, guess who will become suspect number one in that lawyer's murder?"

Louis was an idiot, and Grant didn't want him saying another word until the cops arrived. Not another—

"I mean, you get pregnant by the guy, so that had to mean something, right?"

Pregnant.

Grant's heartbeat stilled in that moment, then started racing in a triple-time rhythm. His gaze flew to Scarlett. All the color had fled from her cheeks.

"No wonder good old Eric flipped out when he heard the news. And after I told him, he said he was going to see *you*, McGuire. Now I'm wondering…just how did that little meeting go? Especially since Eric Turner is the one who wound up dead."

"Grant…" Scarlett's voice was a whisper.

"Be careful, sweet thing," Louis warned her. "From what I can tell, you don't fall for the safe ones. And you're staring right at a man who has killed plenty of times." Louis paused a beat. "I guess the big question is…did he just kill…for you?"

Chapter Four

Scarlett fought to keep her emotions in check. She was back at the police station—big surprise there. Back in an interrogation room, and her lawyer was outside, his raised voice carrying easily through the shut door.

He wanted the case against her to be dismissed.

The prosecutor wasn't ready for that move, not yet. That would be why all the arguing was occurring.

Detective Shayne Townsend had brought Louis in for questioning. He'd confiscated all Louis's photographs, videos and notes about her.

And about Grant.

The door opened and she tensed as Grant stepped in. There was no emotion on his stony face, but his eyes glittered with fury.

She rose on shaky legs. "Grant…"

He marched toward her, shook his head. "Not here," he said quietly. His gaze cut to the right, to the mirror that she knew was really set up for two-way observation. Another room was located behind that glass, a space for the cops to use as they viewed interrogations. Were cops in there even now, watching them?

He hadn't talked to her, not since they'd arrived at the station. She was almost afraid of the conversation that would happen between them, because the fury in his eyes seemed to be directed straight at her.

I never told him. There just...never seemed a point. Why hurt him? She'd carried the pain fine on her own.

The door opened once more. Pierce Jennings stood there, and her lawyer looked pleased. Well, as pleased as it was possible for him to look. Normally, he was in what she thought of as "shark mode." Jennings was considered to be the best criminal defense attorney in the Austin area—and he had that reputation because he would do anything necessary for his clients.

"Am I clear?" Scarlett asked, the hope making her voice crack a bit.

Pierce hesitated then shook his head. "Not yet, but this new evidence sure did blow a hole in the prosecutor's case."

She wanted the case to vanish.

Pierce glanced toward Grant. "I'd heard you were a good PI. Seems the rumors weren't wrong."

Grant inclined his head. No change of expression crossed his face.

"But, uh..." Pierce coughed a bit "...in light of some of the...notes in Louis East's case files, you might need to stay away from my client for a while. I'd advise that you put some distance between the two of you."

Grant's brows climbed.

The lawyer exhaled slowly. He'd shut the interrogation room door behind him. Scarlett knew the cops couldn't monitor them through that two-way mirror, not when she was having a talk with her attorney. For the moment, they were safe to speak freely.

"I didn't realize just how...close you two were." Pierce's gaze darted between Grant and Scarlett. "If I had, then I would've recommended distance from the beginning. Immediately rushing off with an old lover *doesn't* look good, no matter how you spin it."

"I'm her *friend*," Grant said, stretching the word for emphasis.

Pierce let his doubt show. "Are you? Is that really what you want to call it?"

Grant growled.

But Pierce wasn't done. "Fine. Whatever. Semantics. If you truly *are* her friend, then give her some distance. You've helped enormously on this case already. You've been a good *friend*. Now give her some space. Let's see what move the prosecutor makes next. Then we can re-evaluate."

Scarlett crossed her arms over her chest. "Do you think we can truly get this case dismissed?"

Pierce nodded. "You have a rock-solid alibi. The prosecutor is furious right now, but she's going to have to back down. It's only a matter of time."

Hope began to burn brighter inside Scarlett.

Pierce walked toward her. He put his hands on her shoulders and squeezed. "Everything is okay now."

She wanted to believe that.

"You two should leave separately," Pierce directed with a slow nod. "We have to stop the suspicion from mounting about the two of you right away—"

"The suspicion?" Scarlett interrupted.

His lips thinned. "You have an alibi now. Grant here doesn't. The prosecutor may try to spin this as a case where your lover—"

"He's *not*!" Scarlett declared instantly. Grant hadn't been her lover in a very long time.

"—killed your fiancé in a jealous rage."

Those words stole her breath. "Grant wasn't jealous. We'd had no contact in years."

Pierce started to speak, then paused. He still held her shoulders as he glanced over at Grant. "I need to speak privately with my client. Don't worry, I'll see that she gets home safely." It was an obvious dismissal.

But Grant didn't leave. His eyes locked on Scarlett and he headed toward her, while Pierce nervously backed away.

At first, she almost thought that Grant would pull her into his arms. That he would hold her tightly.

Then she saw the fury in his gaze. All the McGuires had those same green eyes, but not all their eyes appeared to glow with rage when they were mad. Only Grant seemed to manage that.

"Grant..."

"We *will* be talking soon, Scarlett. This isn't over."

A promise. Or a threat?

He strode from the room, tension evident in every line of his hard body.

Neither she nor Pierce spoke until the interrogation room door closed behind Grant. Her heartbeat kept racing.

"Well..." Pierce exhaled heavily. "He is as...intense as they say."

Understatement. He was more than *intense*.

Pierce's hand brushed her arm again. "I need you to be careful."

Not again with this. "I'm not involved with Grant! He's *not* my lover—"

Pierce shook his head. "Louis was clear on that. You two haven't been involved in years, but..." His head came closer to hers. "He's been following you. Louis said he caught sight of Grant McGuire watching you several times."

What? That didn't make any sense.

"Louis told Eric Turner about the guy…about him appearing at restaurants you were at. About even seeing him outside your school."

Impossible. Grant wouldn't…wouldn't *stalk* her.

"And when Louis found out about the pregnancy…"

Her lips pressed into a tight line.

"He told Eric about that, too. Louis swears that Eric was planning to confront Grant. To find out what the hell was really happening."

Nothing was happening.

When Pierce's fingers curled under her chin, she realized she was staring down at the floor. He tilted her head up, forcing her to look into his eyes. "I'm trying to get McGuire to stay away," he told her, "because I'm worried."

Worried they might cause suspicion.

"You didn't kill Eric Turner, but someone did…and Grant McGuire knows how to kill. He's done it before, and I think, if he were pushed hard enough, he wouldn't hesitate to do it again."

She shook her head. "Grant was a soldier, he wasn't—"

"He was black ops. I tried to look into his military records, and I got shut down, fast. The man has secrets, and I think we're both better off not knowing them." Her lawyer's hand fell away. "Just as I think you're better off staying away from him."

All of this was just…wrong. "Grant helped me." He'd been the one she turned to when she'd been at her most desperate. "He'd never hurt me."

"Are you so sure about that? Because when he left here, there sure seemed to be a whole lot of rage riding that man."

A shiver skated down her spine. She'd been wrong

about a lover once before, a long time ago. But, no, she *couldn't* be wrong about Grant. *He wouldn't hurt me.*

"We're getting these charges dropped. We *will* prove your innocence." Pierce's solemn stare held hers. "But for your own safety, stay away from Grant McGuire, okay? Just until we find out more."

But she knew what he was really saying. *Stay away... until we find out if he killed Eric Turner.*

The chill she felt sank all the way into her bones.

No, no, no!

He watched as Scarlett left the station. The cops let her just waltz right out the front door. All because that idiot Louis East had simply handed over his files to them.

And now the police were starting to think that Scarlett was innocent. A victim.

They were so blind. Scarlett had never been a victim.

Reporters were shouting questions at her as she walked down the station's steps, but she ignored them and ducked into a cab, which raced away. The swarm turned back toward the cops— toward Detective Shayne Townsend. They were eager for more details. Knowing reporters, the more scandalous or grisly the story, the better. *If it bleeds, it leads.* Yes, he knew the old motto.

There was plenty of blood soaking this murder case.

His gaze slid around the police station. None of the journalists were paying him any attention, not when Townsend was up there, playing to the cameras. While they were all distracted, he needed to get—

Louis.

He saw the man sliding out of the shadows near the right side of the police station. Louis was doing his best to avoid that throng of reporters.

They don't see you, but I do.

His head tilted as he studied Louis East. The man had made too many revelations. And if he was left loose... hell, he could still be holding tight to some secrets. Secrets he'd spill at the wrong time.

So he followed Louis through the dark streets and the narrow alleys. The PI didn't bother with a cab. He was intent on slipping away into the night.

But I won't lose you.

Then Louis rounded a corner.

He followed close behind and—

"You think you can sneak up on me?" Louis lunged for him. Ah, so the PI wasn't as clueless as he seemed.

He dodged the blow and came up fast. Not with a punch of his own, but with a hard stab of his knife.

The knife sank into Louis's side.

"Yes," he said simply, as the PI's eyes widened in shock and pain. "I think I can."

HER LITTLE CONDO was dark. Pitch-black. Scarlett rushed around inside, turning on all the lights as quickly as she could because she hated that enveloping darkness. Oddly, the place felt cold, when it was eighty degrees outside. No, it wasn't just her home that was cold. *She* still felt cold.

She couldn't seem to shake the bone-deep chill.

The den was now lit up, the soft lights glowing. She hurried into her bedroom. Walked into the darkness and quickly flipped up the light switch.

Then she screamed when she saw the man in there. The man who'd been waiting in the dark.

"Scarlett..."

Her hand had grabbed the doorframe in a death grip.

Grant shook his head as he eased toward her. "It's all right. It's just me."

That was the problem.

He's in my bedroom.

"You shouldn't be here. Pierce said—" *Too much.*

"I came up the fire escape. Don't worry, none of your neighbors saw me. I know how to get in a place without being spotted. Ranger training."

She glanced toward her bedroom window. It was open—open to the fire escape, which led to the street below. That would explain why he was in her room, but...

"Why are you here at all?"

His gaze held hers. A muscle flexed in his jaw. "I think you know."

She didn't want to talk about this. She wanted to talk about *anything* but this. "Grant..."

"Was Louis lying?"

"No." Her voice was so soft. He was close enough to touch her now, but he didn't.

"You were pregnant...with *my* baby?"

This time, she didn't speak. Scarlett nodded.

"You never told me!" It was a thundering accusation. She flinched.

"Ten years...*ten years*...and you never told me?" He caught her arms then, pulling her up against him in a grip that was too tight. *"Why?"*

"Because you were gone." Her quiet voice was a direct contrast to the lethal fury of his. "You were gone and the baby was gone, and there was no point in making you—in making you hurt the way I did." She'd grieved enough for them both.

"Scarlett..."

"Something went wrong. It wasn't meant to be," she whispered. "That's what the doctor told me when I lost the baby. It was early, around eight weeks." As if being "early" had helped. The doctor had seemed to think it would, but he'd been wrong. She sucked in a deep breath and tried to keep her voice steady as she said, "It…happens. More than you probably think." Another line from the doctor, words that had been branded in her memory. "Things just…go wrong."

But to lose Grant, then the baby…the baby she'd discovered so soon after she'd said goodbye to Grant…

I lost them both, too close together. I felt like I was losing everything back then.

He never eased his hold on her. "Why didn't you tell me?"

"You were gone…"

"Ten. Years."

Right. She could have told him at some point. "Why? There wasn't anything you could do. The baby was gone. You and I—we were over."

"Were we?"

Her gaze searched his. "You walked away, remember?"

His jaw hardened. "And when I came back, less than a year later, you were with someone else."

Now she was the one reeling in shock. She'd been at college in Georgia then. How would he have known about her and Ian? *Ian…* She tried never to think of him.

"I heard you were going to marry that one, too," Grant snarled. "But that didn't work, did it?"

"I was never going to marry Ian." She'd tried too hard to get away from him. Ian and his charm. He'd pulled her in, seemed to sense how broken she'd felt.

And I was so blind I almost didn't see him for what he was.

"That's not what he told me, not when I came to your dorm room and found him waiting inside."

"Wait, you came to the university?"

He freed her and stepped back. Put some fast distance between them. "I needed to see you. But he told me that you two were getting married. It had only been a year, Scarlett. One damn year, and you'd already moved on. Already replaced me." His laughter was bitter. "So much for love."

"No." The one word held her own fury. "You don't get to say that to me." She'd been through her own hell over the years and she'd come through it, stronger. She'd had to be stronger. "I wasn't the one who left you. I was the one there on that hot summer day, offering you everything I had." It hadn't been enough. She'd never been enough for him. "Ian was lying to you. Turned out he did that. A lot. We were dating. I was already trying to pull away. I had no plans to marry him." Not when she still closed her eyes at night and saw Grant.

And I see you to this day.

"He never told me that you came to my dorm." But Ian had been so good at his deceptions. His little games. "Why…why were you there?"

"Because I needed you." Bitterness turned his voice into a low rasp. "That's the thing, no matter how much time passes, no matter what happens in my life…*I need you.*"

Her pulse was racing.

"I would have loved the baby."

She had to blink because moisture filled her eyes. "I know."

"If he'd…if she'd…if the *baby* had made it, would you have ever told me?"

The accusation hurt. "Yes." Her hands had fisted at her sides.

Grant's head cocked as he studied her. "I used to know you so well. I thought, despite everything, that I still did. But when I look at you now, I can't tell for certain if you're lying to me or not."

"You can't say that to me." But he just had. "You're the one who's been following me." According to Louis. "You're the one—"

He was in front of her in an instant. She retreated, and her back hit the wall. His hands came up, not touching her, but caging her as his palms flattened on the wall. "I haven't followed you."

"East said you had. That you'd been at the same restaurants…"

A snarl broke from Grant. "Coincidence. I looked you up twice and saw you with Eric while I was out."

"My school—"

"I was working a case." Grant's voice was flat. "I wasn't following you." His eyes narrowed. "Is that what you're thinking? That I've been following you? Stalking you? You're the one who came to *me*, Scarlett. The one who needed *me*, and I helped you, no questions asked."

He had. He'd been there when she needed a friend most. But…he wasn't a friend.

He'd always been more.

He leaned nearer. Their bodies brushed. Their mouths were so close. The anger that had been between them was changing. Shifting. Becoming something else entirely.

"Knew for years…" His words were a rumble. "Knew I should stay away from you. If I ever got close again, I understood what would happen."

She didn't understand. "What would happen?"

His eyes were on her mouth. "This."

He lowered his head more, closed that last bit of precious distance between them, and kissed her.

The years fell away in that moment. The fears. The anger. Everything vanished.

It was just as it had been so long ago. The chemistry. The desire. The white-hot need that electrified her. His lips weren't hesitant on hers. There was no gentle coaxing. No getting-to-know-you hesitation.

His mouth locked on hers. His tongue thrust past her lips. He kissed her like a man desperate to taste his lover. Like a man who knew that lover well.

Because he did.

Her hands rose and flattened on his chest. She could feel the power beneath her touch—the steely muscles. He'd always been so strong. And he'd always tasted so good.

She rose onto her toes, trying to get closer to him. How many nights had she dreamed about him? Too many to count.

His hands weren't on the wall any longer. They were curling around her hips. Pulling her against the hard, hot cradle of his thighs.

He wanted her. She could feel the heavy length of his arousal. And despite everything, Scarlett had never stopped wanting him.

His mouth pulled from hers, but he didn't let her go. He started kissing a sensual path down her neck. Licking, caressing and making her heartbeat thunder in her chest and drum in her ears.

There were a million reasons why she should back away from him right then.

But her hands just rose up and curled around his shoulders to hold him tightly.

I want this. I need him.

So when he lifted her and carried her toward the bed, she didn't say a word to stop him. He lowered her slowly and kissed her again. Only Grant kissed her that way. With such stark desire and a need unchecked by anything.

She helped him to push up his shirt. When he tossed it aside and the light hit his chest, a soft gasp escaped her.

There were scars on his skin. From…bullets? A knife attack? Both? The scars were thin, white, old, but they still frightened her. Especially the long one that was so close to his heart.

"They don't matter." His voice was even deeper. "Nothing matters right now but you." He caught the hem of her top and pulled it over her head.

Her shirt joined his on the floor.

Then they were on the bed. He unhooked her bra, put his mouth over her breast. Tasted her. When his tongue touched her, she arched toward him. So eager. So ready to just be with him again. Her fear had disappeared. The past few days, the nightmares—they were gone in that instant.

There was only desire.

Soon, there would be only pleasure.

Everything else could be forgotten, just for a time.

Her hips pushed against his. She still had on her pants. Her shoes were long gone. He wore jeans. She wanted them off. She couldn't touch him enough. His skin was so warm. His muscles flexed against her.

He was kissing her, stroking her skin. His mouth blazed a path down her stomach, and her breath choked out. His fingers slid toward the button of her pants.

And he stopped.

Scarlett pushed up onto her elbows. "Grant?"

His fingers flattened against her. "This will change us."

She needed him. She didn't want to think or talk about the future. Scarlett only wanted to feel.

"I won't be able to go back again. Neither will you."

She licked her lips and tasted him.

Desire had tightened his face. Made his eyes burn with passion. Those eyes were raking over her body, lingering on her breasts. "So beautiful…"

She thought he was perfect. Her hand lifted to trace the scar near his heart. When he slid back, she was the one to rise up on her knees. She put her mouth against that scar and tenderly kissed the mark. Scarlett wished that she could wipe away all his pain.

"Scarlett…you're taking a dangerous path…"

She touched another scar, then one lower, edging around his ribs. He slid back even more and let her lean over him. Her fingers whispered over every wound, and then her lips followed. Feathering lightly over the scars that marked him. Acknowledging the battles that had changed him.

Another scar, about two inches long, ran above the top of his jeans. Her hair brushed over his chest as she bent and pressed her lips to that line.

"Scarlett…"

There was something different about her name then. She looked up and saw Grant's control shatter right before her eyes. There was no other word for it but *shatter*.

In a flash, she was on her back in that bed. Her clothes were gone. His, too. He kept one hand on her thigh even as he took care of their protection.

He continued touching her, as if he was afraid that she might try to escape. But she wouldn't have left. There was no way that she *could* have. She needed him too desperately.

He settled between her thighs. His fingers parted her and she felt him push inside her core.

They'd been together before. Special, sensual meetings the summer she'd graduated high school—before that last date by the lake. He'd been her first. He'd taught her so much about pleasure. She remembered every lesson.

He thrust into her.

Their eyes held.

"Grant..."

He withdrew. Thrust again. The rhythm wasn't slow. The need had crested too fast for them. Everything was so intense—so wild. Her legs rose around him. She held him tightly. Her nails dug into his shoulders as the pleasure built and built.

There was no awkwardness. No hesitations.

Their bodies met again and again.

He kissed her, caressed her. Drove her to the very edge of desire—

And then the release hit her. So strong and consuming that she could only gasp his name.

She remembered pleasure.

She hadn't remembered getting *lost* in him.

But she felt lost then. Because the world spun away and all she could do was hold on to Grant as her body trembled and the waves of release rolled through her again and again. And Grant was with her, growling out her name. Holding her just as fiercely, as the pleasure lashed him, as well.

Her gasping breaths filled the air. Her drumming heartbeat seemed to echo in her ears. And Grant...

He carefully lifted his body up and braced his weight so he didn't crush her into the mattress. Grant gazed down at her. "The memories were wrong. It wasn't like it was back then."

Back then...when she'd been so unsure, caught up in her first love.

This isn't about love. This time is about need. A desire too long unchecked.

"It's not like that now." His lips brushed hers. "It's even better."

And the pleasure was still pulsating through her. This…this was more than she'd expected, and in that moment, her emotions seemed too raw and exposed.

He was staring into her eyes. What did he see? What was she revealing?

"I hope you know," he told her, his voice a sensual rumble, "you and I are just getting started."

SHE WAS ASLEEP.

Grant turned his head and gazed at Scarlett. The moonlight spilled through her window, illuminating the delicate curves of her face. She was naked, covered only by the thin sheet.

His arm was beneath her head. She'd fallen asleep with him. She'd always been too trusting.

Part of him wanted to stay there with her. He'd needed her for so long. Her sweet vanilla scent was on him, and he'd done his best to leave his mark on her.

He'd tried to explain to Scarlett how he felt, but in the heat of the moment, he wasn't sure she'd fully understood what was happening.

She would.

Slowly, carefully, he eased from the bed. She never stirred. He stood there a moment, gazing down at her and remembering the past. But the past was over.

She wasn't the same person.

Neither was he.

He pulled on his clothes. Spared her one last glance, then he left, slipping away down her fire escape and vanishing into the night.

Chapter Five

Grant found Sullivan at his brother's usual hangout, a run-down bar on the edge of town. One with darkened windows and an exterior that appeared to be a day away from falling down.

He was in the back of the joint, a whiskey in front of him as he slouched in the booth. When Grant approached, Sullivan lifted a brow.

"I heard that your lady appears to be innocent." He raised his drink. Saluted. "Guess that has you feeling mighty fine right about now."

Grant would have been feeling better if he'd still been in bed with Scarlett. But he had business to take care of.

Family...you think you can trust them. Then you learn they've been lying to you for years. "You knew," he said flatly as he glowered at his brother.

Sullivan downed his whiskey. "That she hadn't killed that stuffed shirt Eric? Well, yeah, okay, so I figured she probably hadn't gone after him with the knife. The two of you together like that—it caught me off guard and I shot off at the mouth." He rolled his shoulders. "I mean... that knife attack hardly seems her style—"

Grant's fist hit the table. "The baby."

Sullivan slowly lowered the empty glass.

"You were still at home when I left." Sullivan had

joined the marines a good year and a half after that. "You were here. You knew what was happening, didn't you?" Sullivan had always been the brother who knew everything because he seemed to keep tabs on everyone. "Before I left," Grant continued, his voice roughening, "I asked you to look out for her."

"That you did." No emotion entered Sullivan's voice. *"You didn't tell me about the baby!"*

Sullivan stared down at his empty glass. "What do you want to hear me say? That I'm sorry? I made a judgment call. You were fighting for your life over there. You needed to focus on the mission."

"And she needed me."

Sullivan still wasn't looking at him. "Scarlett came to the ranch as soon as she found out she was pregnant. I heard her talking to Mom and Dad. She told them about the baby. She wanted them to know their grandchild."

Those words gutted him. *They knew, too...they knew?*

"They didn't have the chance to tell you. Scarlett lost the baby that very night."

There was something about Sullivan's voice...a rough edge...and Grant knew. His eyes widened. "You were there."

Sullivan shrugged. "You asked me to watch her. She'd just finished waiting tables at that old restaurant, The Mill, when it—it happened..."

Grant remembered that place. Scarlett had been working there to earn extra money for college. He'd gone in a few times, always enjoying the way her face lit up when she saw him.

That doesn't happen any longer. When she looks at me now, she's so guarded.

And he always caught the shadow of pain in her eyes. "I didn't think she should be alone at the hospital.

Didn't think you'd want her alone." Sullivan's fingers tapped on the tabletop. "So, yeah, I was there." He glanced up and Grant's body stiffened when he saw the anger glinting in his brother's eyes. "What do you want to hear now? That she cried? She did. That she begged the doctor, that she told him again and again how much she loved the baby? She did. And you know what he told her?" His lips twisted. "Something went wrong."

Those had been Scarlett's exact words to him before.

Sullivan tossed some cash down on the table and rose. But he didn't walk away. He kept his glare on Grant. "You two hurt each other enough before. You came in this time, you played the hero. You got her clear…"

The charges hadn't been dropped, not yet.

"So now you need to be smart. Walk away."

Grant didn't want to walk away from her. He couldn't.

"I'll never forget the way she looked in that hospital." Sullivan's voice had lowered. "And you know what else I won't forget? The way you looked when you came back from that trip to Georgia."

When he'd been so desperate to see Scarlett and he'd followed her to the university. Only she hadn't been in that dorm room.

Ian lied, Scarlett's voice whispered through his mind.

"You went out, got so drunk you could barely move, and then you started picking a fight with the first low-life you saw."

No, it hadn't been just any lowlife.

"That guy who used to tease Scarlett so much because her dad cut out on her family. He made the mistake of saying her name…" Sullivan exhaled. "I had to pull you off him. You were out of control. *Because of her.*"

Grant didn't speak.

"The two of you are a dangerous combination. So be safe this time and walk away."

He shook his head. "I can't." It was too late for that. He turned away, but Sullivan caught his arm.

"We have enough crap happening right now," Sullivan said, voice rasping. "After all this time, we still don't have the SOBs who killed our parents. And Ava…you know she's not the same. She's been too fragile since then. We have to focus on our family. We have to protect them." His hold tightened. "You and Scarlett are trouble that we can't handle now."

It wasn't about making a choice between Scarlett and his family. "I know my responsibilities."

"Do you? Because I'm worried about you, bro…worried about the way you look at Scarlett. Worried about—"

Grant knocked Sullivan's hand away. "How do I look at her?"

"Like you can't live without her. Like you'd destroy anyone who tried to take her from you." Sullivan's eyes were narrow. "That's dangerous. She wrecks your control. She always has, and you can't expect me to just stand by while you spiral—"

Grant's laughter cut through his brother's words. Cold, hard laughter. "Don't come between me and Scarlett."

Realization filled Sullivan's eyes. "You've—already?"

Grant's jaw locked. "And don't ever keep a secret about her again. When it comes to Scarlett, I need to know everything." He pulled away from his brother. Took a step—

"Then I guess I should tell you about Ian Lake." His tone was flat. Bitter.

Grant looked back.

"Because I'm sure Scarlett won't tell you about him."

Ian's smiling, pretty boy face flashed through Grant's mind.

"Secrets…" Sullivan muttered. "They have a way of wrecking you."

SOMEONE WAS KNOCKING at her door. Scarlett opened one eye, expecting to see Grant's glorious naked self right beside her in the bed.

He wasn't there.

His pillow was empty.

No glorious, naked body.

Her other eye opened. Her hands stretched out and touched the sheets. They were cold, holding none of his body warmth, as if he'd been gone for too long.

The pounding came again. She sat up, pulling the sheet with her. A quick glance at the nearby clock showed her it was close to 1:00 a.m. Who would be visiting her then?

Grant.

She jumped from the bed. Kept that sheet wrapped around her. Maybe he'd gone out for a minute and now was trying to get back inside. She hurried toward the living room and the front door.

But the pounding had stopped. She started to open the lock, then hesitated. Biting her lip, Scarlett leaned forward and put her eye to the peephole.

She didn't see anyone out there.

But…but someone *had* been there.

Unease slid through her. She turned around, realizing that much of her home was in darkness. She pulled the sheet closer.

Where had Grant gone? Why had he left?

Maybe he'd written her a note. She flipped on the lamp near the couch and turned on the light over her desk in the den.

There were no notes in there. She reached for her phone, thinking she'd call him—

Stop. He left you. Don't give him a desperate call in the middle of the night. He. Left.

As if he hadn't done that before. She shouldn't have been surprised.

She put the phone back on the desk.

She shouldn't have been surprised that he'd slipped away, but she was. She was also hurt.

Her feet were silent as she headed back to her bedroom. It was dark in there, but some moonlight spilled through her window, falling onto the bed.

She put on a loose T-shirt and leggings. Then she slid back into the bed. She could smell Grant there. His rich, masculine scent. And she could still feel him all along her body.

In her.

She squeezed her eyes shut and tried to take some slow, deep breaths.

That was when she heard the creak, a soft creak of wood. It sounded as if it had come from near her window. The window that led out to the fire escape.

It could have been nothing. She lived in an older building. A converted brownstone that had been divided into condo units. She was on the top floor, the third floor.

It could have been nothing...

But then the sound came again. Another creak of her wooden floor. Her eyes flew open.

Grant?

A dark shadow stood at the edge of her bed.

"Grant?" Scarlett whispered, but fear was snaking through her. *Not Grant. Not Grant!*

The shadow lunged toward her, and Scarlett screamed.

GRANT PUSHED HIS brother closer to the back of the bar. "What about Ian?"

"I got curious after your little side trip up to Georgia. I wondered just what had gone wrong."

Grant growled. The guy was testing his patience. Tension had knotted Grant's stomach.

"When I got there, Scarlett was in the hospital."
What?

"See her too much there," Sullivan muttered.

"What had happened to her?"

"Her boyfriend. Seemed he was the jealous type."
Rage twisted in Grant.

"He broke her arm and bruised her ribs. She said he pushed her down the stairs of her dorm. He said she was drinking and fell."

A dull roar filled Grant's ears.

"One of his frat buddies backed him up, claiming that he saw Scarlett drinking, so no charges were filed."

Grant's hands were fists. "Did you talk to Scarlett?"

"No, I talked to that jerk, Ian. I let him know that *nothing* else would happen to her. That he'd stay as far from Scarlett as possible or *he'd* be the one in the hospital. And a broken arm would be the least of his injuries."

Grant's body was actually shaking with the force of his rage. How many more secrets did Scarlett carry? And would they all cut him up like this?

Ian hurt her…I could have stopped that. I could have been right there. I would have knocked that fool—

"Based on the way you acted, I figured you and

Ian had gotten into a fight, and he took his fury out on Scarlett."

"We didn't fight," he said, voice tight. Grant wished they had. He wished he'd stayed in that dorm longer and actually seen Scarlett, talked with her.

"Scarlett? You're looking for my Scarlett?" Ian's pale blue eyes had widened. *"And who the hell are you to be looking for my girlfriend?"*

He'd seen the picture then, behind Ian. A photo on the desk…of Scarlett and Ian.

Grant's voice had been rough when he'd demanded, *"You're with Scarlett?"* But that answer had been obvious, so he'd plowed on. *"I'm Grant McGuire. An old friend. I have to see her."*

Ian had recognized his name. *"You're no friend. Scarlett is done with you. Her future is with me. A future we're already planning."* And the guy had smirked. *"We're looking at rings this weekend."*

Grant couldn't even remember what he'd said after that. He'd felt foolish for chasing her across all those miles to Georgia. He'd been mooning over her for months, and she'd already hooked up with someone else.

He'd been so furious to see that little jerk in her room, talking as if he had some kind of right to Scarlett.

And I'd been so angry at her because she wasn't as torn up as I was. Because she'd moved on, and I couldn't get her out of my mind.

"You keep too many secrets," Grant told his brother as he tried to push back his anger. "If you'd just said—"

"By the time I got to Georgia, you were already on your way back to the Middle East. You had a rescue mission there and your team was counting on you."

They had been, but Scarlett had been hurting. Grant hadn't been there for her. Again. No wonder there was so much pain in her eyes when she looked at him. He did nothing but let her down.

"You told me," Sullivan said. "Before you left for that mission, you told me that you were done with Scarlett Stone."

Such a lie. He'd known it even as he'd spoken those words. She'd gotten past his guard, when he should have been more vigilant. *I'll never be done with her.*

"You need to be done," Sullivan said flatly. "You let that woman get too much of a hold on you. I'll never have that weakness."

Never say never, brother.

But Sullivan didn't let anyone close. Grant lifted his chin. "Scarlett and I aren't done." They had just found their way back to one another. This time, though, he'd get things right with her. He'd be damned if he repeated the mistakes from his past.

"I was afraid you'd say that."

Grant glared at him. "I don't need you to keep an eye on Scarlett. I've got her from here on out."

"Whatever you say." His brother shouldered past him. Controlled, dangerous Sullivan. The man had too many shadows on his soul, and with every day that passed, Grant often felt as if Sullivan pulled further away from him and the rest of the family.

Sully. He'd been so carefree as a boy. But then everything had changed…overnight.

Sullivan stopped, pausing near a booth about five feet away. His back was tense. "You ever think it was because of us?"

Grant frowned.

"You made enemies, I made enemies. The twins…hell, we all stir up plenty of trouble." Sullivan looked back at him. "Five years have passed, and there are *no* new clues about our parents' murder. The crime was so perfect."

Too perfect.

"What if it was because of us? What if someone hurt them to get at us?"

It was a question that haunted Grant, and he'd been tracking down every lead he could find in the past five years in order to answer that question. But so far, he'd turned up nothing.

There was no reason for the crime. No motive that he could see.

On the night of November twenty-eighth, hell had come calling to the ranch that Grant had once called home. A ranch that had been in his family for over one hundred years—ever since his great-grandfather had emigrated from Ireland.

Intruders had broken into the house. Those men had proceeded to shoot their victims, first Grant's mother, then his father, at point-blank range. They'd ransacked the house, looking for something.

We're just lucky they didn't kill Ava.

"We're going to find them." That was why he'd come home. To bring justice to his parents. To protect Ava.

Ava still won't look me in the eye. She flinches whenever anyone gets too close to her.

"I've got enough sins on my soul," Sullivan said as he rolled his shoulders. "I don't want that one, too."

"We'll find them." Grant had been making that same promise for years.

"And when we do?" His brother's gaze held his. "Do you play hero again? Or do we punish them? Because doing the right thing…some days, I'm not even sure what that is anymore."

Sullivan walked away, leaving Grant in the bar.

He glanced down at his clenched hands.

The right thing...

Some days, he wasn't sure what that was, either.

Grant made his way out of the bar, but by the time he got to the street, Sullivan was long gone.

SCARLETT GRABBED THE lamp on the nightstand and threw it at her attacker. But he didn't stop. The dark shadow surged toward her. Gloved fingers wrapped around her ankles and jerked her toward the edge of the bed.

She aimed for his face, intending to drag her claws across his skin or gouge his eyes but—*He's wearing a ski mask.* She felt the soft fabric against her fingertips.

And she also felt the cold touch of a knife press into her side. Her T-shirt had bunched up in the struggle, and the knife's blade nicked her skin.

Scarlett froze.

An image of Eric's body flashed into her mind. The terrible wounds. The blood.

The knife pressed harder against her. "Please," she whispered, "don't hurt me."

He laughed.

And a pounding reverberated through her place. A pounding? *Someone was at the front door again.*

Her eyes widened. One of her attacker's hands was on her leg now and one held the knife. *You should have covered my mouth—your mistake!* "Help!" Scarlett screamed at the top of her lungs. "Please, help me!"

She shoved against the intruder and that blade slid down. She felt its sting against her skin—harder and deeper this time—and something wet dripped across her side. *Blood, my blood.*

There was a crash in the other room.

Her attacker let her go. He jumped away from the bed

and ran for the window and the fire escape. She reached out, trying to grab him, but he was too fast.

Footsteps thundered in the den.

"Help!" she yelled again as she staggered out of the bed. She was bleeding. Her hand covered her side just as the lights in her bedroom flashed on.

Detective Townsend stood there, a gun in his right hand, his eyes wild. *"Scarlett?"*

She pointed toward the fire escape. The window leading out there—that window was open, but there was no sign of her attacker. "He's running!" Her voice was too high. Too scared. "He had a knife!"

Shayne lunged for the window.

Get him. Get him!

Her hand was still pressed to her side, and the blood kept dripping through her fingers. Shayne leaped through the narrow window opening and gave chase, rushing down the fire escape.

She stumbled toward the window. Adrenaline and terror pulsed through her, a combination that left her shaking. She could see Shayne below, but there was no sign of the other man.

He'd laughed...

And that laughter had seemed strangely familiar.

GRANT DROVE BACK to Scarlett's place, his hands too tight around the steering wheel. His brother's words kept replaying in his head.

Grant had never wanted to hurt Scarlett, and never wanted her to be hurt *because* of him. When he looked back over his life, his best moments had been with her and—

Flashing blue lights illuminated the front of Scarlett's

building. Uniformed police officers were searching the area with flashlights.

An ambulance had parked to the right, near the curb. *What in the hell?*

He slammed on his brakes and leaped from his SUV even as fear grabbed hold of his heart. He ran toward the building's entrance, but a uniformed cop stepped in his path, blocking his way.

"Who are you, buddy? You live here?"

Clenching his teeth and trying to choke back his fear, Grant said, "My girlfriend does." Girlfriend wasn't so much a stretch, not after what they'd shared that night.

"Girlfriend, huh?" The questioning voice came from behind him. He whirled around and saw Shayne standing there, with his arms crossed over his chest. His badge was clipped to his belt. "And here I thought Scarlett Stone was just your client. Interesting that you have such a personal relationship with her."

Snarling, Grant advanced on the detective. "What's happening? Where's Scarlett?" He'd been gone for only an hour. One hour. He'd planned to slip back before she woke up.

Shayne's head inclined toward the ambulance. "They're getting her patched up."

They're getting her—

Grant ran to the vehicle. Sure enough, he saw Scarlett sitting in the back. Two EMTs were beside her. One was putting a thick white bandage on her lower right side.

"Ma'am, are you sure you don't want to come to the hospital?"

She shook her head. "You said I didn't need stitches. It's just a scratch."

Grant realized then that only one of the men with her

was actually an EMT. The other guy looked as if he was collecting evidence…from beneath her nails?

"Scarlett." Her name came out too gruff and hard. Her head whipped toward him. "What happened, baby?" The endearment slipped out before he could stop it.

"Grant." The inside of the ambulance was well lit, so he could easily see the paleness of her skin. And the residual fear in her eyes.

He wanted to be in that ambulance, holding her. He stepped forward.

Shayne's hand settled on his shoulder. Hard. "I can tell you what happened. An intruder in a ski mask broke into her unit. He slipped up on the fire escape."

The same way I entered.

"He had a knife. One he used on her."

The crime scene tech finished up with Scarlett. He slid from the ambulance. The EMT backed up. Scarlett sat there, staring down at her hands.

Grant couldn't take his gaze off the bandage or her bloodstained T-shirt.

"I heard her scream," Shayne said, his eyes hard with the memory. "If I hadn't…well, it seems her neighbors, the Hills, are out of town on a business trip, and Kylie Jones was pulling an all-nighter at her shop. No one else would have been there. No one else would have heard her."

She'd be dead.

"Scarlett." Grant's voice wasn't hard this time. It was desperate.

She turned her head to meet his gaze. "I thought you were there." Her voice was lost. "Then…later…for an instant, I thought he *was* you, until he attacked me."

She slowly climbed from the ambulance. Her bloody shirt fell down to cover her bandage. Reporters were there now; he could see them watching with avid eyes. He shouldn't give them any more fuel to add to the already raging fire of Scarlett's story. He should stay in control.

He should.

A tear leaked down her cheek.

He jerked away from Shayne and pulled Scarlett into his arms. "I'm sorry, baby," he whispered as he held her tight. He could feel her heart racing like mad, pounding too fast. "I'm so sorry I wasn't there."

Her arms locked around him.

"That brings up an interesting question." Shayne had worked with him before. They were friends, but Shayne didn't exactly sound friendly right then. "Where were you, Grant?"

He didn't let Scarlett go. "I was with my brother Sullivan at the Gray Canyon." Grant knew Shayne would recognize the name of the place.

The detective nodded, but his expression was still guarded. "I'm sure Sullivan and others at the bar can back up that alibi?"

He needed an alibi? Grant's body stiffened. Keeping his arm around Scarlett, he glanced back at the detective. "They can confirm it," he promised. "And if you need an alibi confirmed, that tells me you let the attacker get away."

Shayne's chin jutted up. "He won't get far."

Damn it.

A slight tremble shook Scarlett's body. Reporters were filming them. Some were snapping pictures. "You heard her scream," Grant said, repeating Shayne's words. "It's long after midnight. Why were you outside Scarlett's door?"

The blue lights were still flashing.

"Because I was looking for you and Scarlett. I thought you'd both want to know…"

"Know what?" Grant pressed, when the detective's words trailed away.

Shayne was watching him with a too-assessing stare. "That Louis East is dead. We found his body earlier tonight. Someone stabbed him and left his corpse in an alley."

Chapter Six

Sometimes a nightmare wouldn't end. No matter how hard you tried to wake yourself up, it just wouldn't happen.

Scarlett felt as if she were in one of those terrible dreams right then.

The sun was up; she could see the dawn light spreading across the sky. But the nightmare wasn't over.

"Louis East gave the cops his evidence before..." Grant cleared his throat. "Before his death. That evidence can still help to clear you."

They were back in Grant's house. On his deck. She should have felt safe there.

She didn't.

Scarlett glanced over at him. He wore a pair of low-slung jeans and his hair was mussed, though not from her fingers this time. He'd spent the past few hours either online or on his phone—pushing his brothers to help him gather evidence on a case that was spinning out of control. And as they'd dug for information, his fingers had raked through his thick hair.

It was a Saturday morning. She wouldn't find out anything else on her case until Monday. But she knew the press would be filled with all kinds of stories and speculations. The media would be going crazy.

"We don't know that his death is connected to your case," Grant said slowly.

She had to laugh at that. He was trying to make her feel, what—better? That wasn't happening. Her laugh sounded bitter, even to her own ears. "Eric was stabbed to death. I was attacked by a man with a knife, and *the same night*, Louis East was killed. I think it's pretty clear all of that is connected." Connecting those dots wasn't exactly a hard job. Her breath was ragged as she continued, "Shayne told me that it appeared Louis was attacked less than an hour—*an hour*—after he left the police station. Someone was out there, waiting on him." Stalking him like prey.

Grant closed the distance between them. "The same person who then went to watch your condo?" His fingers curled around her arms.

"The man who waited for you to leave," she whispered, because she'd figured this out in the hours before dawn. "So that he could come after me."

If Shayne hadn't arrived, Scarlett knew she'd be dead. A chill had settled over her, and that chill had been numbing her for hours now. "Why?" She just didn't understand why this was happening.

"We understand the motive, and then we'll find the killer."

Or he'd find her again. She pulled away from Grant and turned back to stare at the sunrise. The world looked so beautiful right then, but there was plenty of evil out there. Evil that often hid in plain sight. "All of the deaths are tied to me. The killer even tried to frame me for Eric's murder."

But when that frame job had started to unravel, when Louis came forward to alibi her...

Did you kill Louis in order to punish him?

"I was looking for enemies that Eric might have." Grant was right behind her. She could feel him there, but he wasn't touching her. "I was looking in the wrong direction."

She didn't want to hear this.

"I should have been looking at enemies you have."

"I'm a schoolteacher. I spend my days with fourth graders." Or she had, but that job wasn't looking secure now. *Once I'm cleared, maybe I can go back.* "I can't think of anyone who would hate me enough to do something like this." She didn't exactly go around trying to anger people.

She had a few friends in Austin. Most were other schoolteachers. *Not* murderers.

"Maybe it's a former lover who's holding a grudge. In cases like this, well, I told you before that knife attacks tend to be more personal. Do you have a lover who…"

Now she did glance back at him. "Who what? Wants me so much he can't let go? Or would rather see me dead than with someone else?" She shook her head. "There have only been three, Grant." Sure, she'd dated plenty of other men, but she hadn't gotten intimately close with them because the connection just hadn't been there—for her or them.

Surprise rippled over his face.

"You didn't have a problem letting me go," she reminded him with a snap in her voice.

"Scarlett…"

She shrugged. She'd just been stating a fact. She didn't need him to try and make excuses at this late date.

"I was with Ian Lake, briefly, when I was in college. We didn't end well." Understatement of the century. "He transferred shortly after our breakup, and I haven't seen him since then. And Eric…well, he's sure not the guilty one, is he?"

The sunlight made Grant's eyes appear brighter. "*Ian*. He hurt you."

She blinked, and understanding settled in for her. "Right…you talked to Sullivan last night." Her eyes narrowed as she thought about the tension she could all but feel crackling in the air around them. "He didn't…just tell you that, did he?"

"Yes."

Ah, that would explain some of the fury she saw in Grant's glittering eyes. "Sullivan is usually pretty good at keeping secrets." He'd kept hers over the years.

Only fair, as she'd kept his, too.

She shrugged, trying to push away that chill. "Ian was a control freak. I got tired of being controlled." And who would *not* be abused. Her father had pushed her mother around a few times before he'd cut and left town. She and her mom had both been glad to see him vanish. And in the years before her mother had passed from cancer… those had been their happiest times.

Scarlett cleared her throat. "I met Ian when I thought I needed someone else to help me move on with my life."

Grant just watched her.

"I knew soon enough that I only needed myself. The last thing I needed was a guy like him."

She realized then that she'd been rubbing her right arm. The arm he'd broken on those stairs. And Grant's watchful stare was focused on it.

She immediately stopped rubbing and dropped her arm to her side.

"Ian and a witness said you were drinking."

Chatty Sullivan. He wasn't usually that way. "Ian had been drinking, and I'd had one glass of wine. Look, the

folks at the hospital did a blood-alcohol test. I was sober."
She'd never drunk to excess—especially not back then,
when the party scene had been new to a fresh-faced Texas
girl. "When I broke up with him, he shoved me."

"Down a flight of stairs."

She could still see his face. Hear his frantic whispers
in her ear. *"I'm sorry, I'm sorry... I'll make it up to you.
Don't tell, Scarlett! Don't tell."*

But she had told.

No one had believed her. The cops had thought that
even with just one glass of wine, she'd simply lost her
footing on the stairs. Especially when Ian had gotten his
buddy to back up his account of that night.

"Where is Ian now?"

Her brows shot up. *Don't know. Don't want to know.*
"It's not like I kept up with him. Seeing him again was
the last thing on my agenda."

"I'll find him."

Her stomach flip-flopped. "Grant..."

"Someone tried to kill you!" There was the fury, biting through his words. "And Ian has a history of hurting
you." The faint lines near Grant's eyes tightened. "I can't
let you get hurt again."

She swallowed. Her side didn't ache this morning.
The wound had been shallow, luckily, hardly more than
a scratch, despite the pain she'd felt at the time. But if
she hadn't gotten away from that man... "Do you think
he'll come after me again?"

Grant didn't answer. But wait, maybe that silence *was*
a response.

"You won't be alone again," he promised.

She wanted to believe him. "You can't stay with me
24-7." He had other clients. Family commitments. He
couldn't drop everything else in his life for her.

"When I'm not with you, one of my brothers will be."

Not Sullivan. Maybe she could put in a request for the twins. Brodie had always been the most lighthearted of the McGuire bunch.

"Until we catch this guy…" Grant's hand rose and the back of his knuckles slid over her cheek. "The McGuires will keep you safe. I swear it."

She tried to lighten the desperate tension around them. "I'm going to owe you so much money when this is all over."

But his face hardened even more. "I already told you, don't worry about the money. This isn't about money."

Her gaze searched his. "Then what is it about?"

"I want another chance."

Her jaw dropped. "What?"

"Me. You. Us. I want us to try again."

She would have backed away, but there was no place to go. She was already pressed up against the wooden railing of the deck. "You decide this now?" Scarlett shook her head. "I don't know if anyone has ever told you this before or not, but you have horrible timing. Like, seriously, the worst timing in the world." She was already guilt-stricken because she'd given in to her need and made love to him two months after Eric's death. She'd broken up with Eric, but—

"I've never wanted another woman the way I want you."

She gave a frantic shake of her head. Grant was trying to take them down a road she wasn't ready to face, not then. "Someone tried to kill me!" She pushed past him. "I can't handle this right now."

"You wanted me last night."

Her steps stumbled to a halt. "Grant, I pretty much always want you." She didn't look back at him. "That doesn't mean I think we can make it together." She hurried forward, heading into the house—and she wasn't especially surprised to find Sullivan waiting in the den. She stumbled to a stop when she saw him. Worry whispered through her. Sullivan was so close to the back deck. Had he overhead them?

"Guess you just let yourself in this time," she finally muttered.

He shrugged. His eyes swept over her. "Heard about the attack last night." He took a step forward. "Are you okay?"

"No." She was far from okay. "I want to find this guy. I want to stop him."

"And then you want to get away from my brother?" His voice was low.

Low enough that Grant didn't overhear? He was still outside, just a few steps behind her.

"Stop telling him my secrets," Scarlett hissed.

But Sullivan shook his head. He lifted a newspaper that she hadn't even noticed in his grip. "Everyone's learning your secrets now."

She took the paper from him, too conscious of Grant now that he'd followed her inside. Scarlett unfolded the paper. The headline was big and bold: Scarlett Stone… Murderer or Victim?

Last night, she'd just been the victim. A photographer had captured an image of her, held tightly in Grant's arms. She looked as if she'd been crying.

I had been.

Her gaze scanned over the article. The reporter had identified Grant. Mentioned him as being both the PI who was intent on proving her innocence and…

Scarlett Stone's high school sweetheart.

Her fingers tightened on the paper.

Reports indicate that Stone was once pregnant with McGuire's child.

She shoved the paper back at Sully. "Isn't there such a thing as patient-doctor confidentiality? How did they learn that?"

"Secrets have a way of getting out." Grant's voice was flat.

Fury pumped through her. If Sully hadn't already told Grant the truth, then Grant would have just discovered one of her most painful secrets by reading about it in the morning paper.

Humiliating. Infuriating.

Sullivan was a slightly rougher version of Grant. His eyes were wilder, his hair dark where Grant's was light, and a graze of stubble already lined his jaw—testament to the long night he must have pulled. With his eyes still on her, he lifted one brow and said, "So if you have any more secrets, now is the time to tell them."

The McGuires already seemed to know everything.

"Because someone is fixated on you," Sullivan continued, "and if we don't figure out who he is, then the guy will just keep coming."

Until I'm dead?

The chill she'd felt for so long deepened even more.

Pregnant?

Scarlett Stone had been pregnant with Grant's child? Rage clawed at his insides.

She was so conniving. Making the world think she was perfect. A victim.

When no, she was the one who'd been destroying lives for so long. The one who needed to be stopped.

I will stop her.

The image of her and Grant McGuire filled the paper.

She looked weak. Delicate. As if she needed someone to protect her.

Lie. Lie. Lie.

That was all Scarlett did. She manipulated men. Tricked them. Made them think that she needed them.

She used them up, and when she was done…

Scarlett just walked away.

You won't walk away this time.

She wouldn't be getting away at all. If jail wasn't in her future…

Then death is waiting.

"I THINK I'M getting far too used to this place," Scarlett murmured as she stared up at the police station. "My home away from home." But Grant realized there was no humor in those grim words.

Only sadness.

Shayne had called him. Asked him to come in with Scarlett once more. There were more questions that the detective wanted to ask.

Always more.

Scarlett's lawyer hurried to greet them.

Pierce took Scarlett's hands as his eyes slid over her. His gaze was dark with concern. "You should have called me," he said. "Right away." The guy was clinging a little too tightly to her. "I didn't find out about your attack until this morning!" Anger sharpened his words.

Grant's eyes narrowed. "She was busy recovering from her attack." He pushed the lawyer back.

"But…but I can use this." Pierce huffed out a breath. "She's attacked, Eric is killed, Louis East is knifed… this is a pattern. Further proof that Scarlett is innocent!"

Pierce Jennings was supposed to be the best criminal

defense attorney in Austin. Based on his court records, the guy sure excelled at getting freedom for his clients.

But Pierce didn't seem to actually care if his clients were innocent or guilty. Grant knew of several guilty men that had walked, thanks to Pierce. He and the attorney had butted heads a few times in the past, and Grant knew that they would clash again in the future.

I care too much if the guilty walk.

Pierce…he was just doing his job.

"We should go inside," Grant muttered. "The detectives are waiting—"

"Scarlett Stone!" It was a roar of fury.

Grant whirled around at the cry. He saw Justin Turner staggering across the street. Car horns blared at the guy. Justin ignored them. His eyes were on Scarlett.

"This isn't good," Pierce said, his nasally voice sharpening.

No, it wasn't good.

Because there was rage in Justin's eyes. His face was bright red and his trembling hands were clenched at his sides.

The guy didn't look like the buttoned-down, controlled lawyer any longer. He looked enraged.

And he was heading right for Scarlett.

Grant stepped in front of her. "You shouldn't be here," he told him.

"Why not?" Justin weaved a bit. Drinking…again? It was barely 8:00 a.m. "The cops called me. Wanted to talk to m-me." His eyes raked over Grant. "You're the one who shouldn't be here, but I guess you just have to stay at her side, right? Seeing as how you two are so…cl-close."

"I'm going to get Detective Townsend," Pierce said, as he turned and hurried up the steps. Leaving them out there.

Leaving Grant to face the man's rage.

"I read the story in the paper," Justin snarled. "You two were l-lovers before. And you're right back with her now, aren't you?"

Grant raised his hands and stepped toward the guy. "You need to calm down."

Justin knocked them aside. "You need to wake up! Don't you s-see what she's doing? She's using you. She's setting this all up to m-make herself look like a victim!" His words were stuttering, slurred.

"Justin…" Scarlett's voice was soft. "I'm so very sorry about Eric—"

"Shut up! Don't you say his name to me!" Justin shouted, then tried to attack her.

Grant wasn't letting that happen. He grabbed the other man, twisted him around, and in an instant, he had Justin's arms pinned behind him. Justin was heaving and shouting, trying to break free, but Grant wasn't letting him go anywhere.

He'd handled men a hundred times stronger than Justin back in his ranger days. There was no way this guy was going to wrestle free from him.

The police station's main doors flew open. Shayne and two uniformed cops rushed down the steps.

Grant put his mouth near Justin's ear. "Don't come at her again. I won't just hold you back next time. I'll be the one attacking you."

As the words sank in, Justin stopped struggling. His head turned and his eyes locked with Grant's.

Satisfied that his message had been received, Grant let him go. The cops were there. Eric's brother would know better than to attack with those particular witnesses.

"It was you," Justin whispered, as if he'd just come to some grand realization.

Grant edged back toward Scarlett. Her lawyer had sure cut and run fast enough. *Way to abandon your client.*

"I thought…I thought she'd done it."

Shayne closed in on Justin, who was really weaving now.

"But it was you. You wanted her b-back. So you killed my brother. Did you kill Louis East, too? That PI who was in the p-paper?"

Shayne took his arm. "You're drunk. I can barely understand a word you're saying and you smell like you bathed in booze."

"Did the—did the PI know? Did East know? Is that why you took him out?"

Grant just shook his head. His gaze met Shayne's. "You need to put him in the drunk tank. He came at Scarlett, tried to hurt her."

"*But you stopped me.* You're always there with her, aren't you?" Justin pointed at Grant. "It was y-you!"

"Scarlett was attacked last night," Shayne said flatly, as he motioned to the other cops to close in on the man.

"Bet he did it," Justin said, his eyes bright now. "Bet he did it to make her scared…to m-make her think she needed him." He was laughing as the uniformed cops led him up the steps. "You're trusting the wrong guy, Scarlett! The wrong one!"

Shayne shook his head as he watched Justin disappear into the station. "So much for interviewing him. I'll have to wait until he sobers up." His gaze slid to Scarlett. "Does he do that a lot?"

"Accuse me of killing his brother? Yes, lots of people accuse me of killing Eric." Her shoulders straightened even as her chin notched up a bit. "He's wrong. They're all wrong."

Shayne absorbed that. And based on the gleam in

his eyes, Grant thought the guy might just be on Scarlett's side.

"Are you okay?" Pierce asked her, sounding out of breath. Probably from all that running up and down the stairs. Running away from the threat.

"Fine." Scarlett's voice was clipped. "Can we just go inside before some reporter starts filming all of this, too?"

"Right." Shayne stepped forward. "I've got some information that I thought you might want to hear."

They were silent as they made their way up the steps and into an interrogation room. Grant could still hear Justin hurling accusations across the police station. Only they weren't against Scarlett any longer.

They're against me.

Shayne shut the door behind them and sealed their group in the small room. "You know that when Eric Turner was killed, we believed his attacker used a vase to hit him over the head, to subdue him so that he fell to the floor before the killer stabbed him."

Scarlett flinched.

"Why are we having this little recap?" Pierce demanded. "If you're wasting our time…"

"I'm not wasting your time," Shayne rushed to assure him.

Pierce didn't appear convinced. "Because I've already got my own medical examiner going back over Eric Turner's case file. He thinks the stab wounds are consistent with a right-handed attacker, and since we've established that Scarlett is left-handed—"

"Take a breath," Shayne told the lawyer.

Pierce's eyes narrowed. His nostrils flared.

"Thank you," Shayne muttered. "Look, the prosecutor is working to get the case against Scarlett dismissed."

She gave a little gasp.

"I'm sure you'll be talking with the prosecutor plenty," Shayne told the lawyer. "But first, I have to deal with the fact that a killer has recently attacked three times here in my town. He went after Eric, he killed East and he got too close to Scarlett last night."

"You think it's the same perp," Grant said flatly.

Shayne nodded. His gaze sharpened on Scarlett. "I need you to walk me through every moment of that attack again, Scarlett."

"I already told you everything—three times!"

"The attacker isn't stopping. He's escalating." Shayne tapped his fingers on the table. "Think about the attack. Did he say anything?"

"He never said a word!" Then her eyelids flickered. "But he laughed. When I tried to fight him, he laughed at me."

Grant couldn't take his eyes off Scarlett.

"I remember thinking that I'd heard him laugh before."

Shayne jumped on that. "You know him?"

"I don't... His laugh was familiar, or at least it seemed familiar, but..." She shook her head. "No, I can't place it. I don't know him."

"When you first saw the guy in your bedroom, you thought he was Grant. That's what you told me last night." He paused. "Why'd you think it was him?"

Her gaze met Grant's. "Because Grant had used the fire escape earlier. He'd been with me when I went to sleep, and I just thought that was him, coming back." Her fingers lightly touched the bandage beneath her shirt. "The guy had big shoulders, broad like Grant's. He was about Grant's height."

"And you knew it wasn't Grant when...?"

"When he lunged for me. He grabbed my leg. His grip

hurt." Her voice softened when she said, "Grant would never hurt me like that."

"Who *would* hurt you?" Shayne asked carefully.

It was the same question that Grant wanted answered. But he already had suspects of his own. Ian Lake. And Justin Turner.

"Start at the beginning," Shayne said as he pulled out a chair. "Tell me about the attack. Every single detail."

"ARE YOU CERTAIN that you feel safe with him?" Pierce asked Scarlett, as they stood on the steps of the police precinct. His eyes were on Grant, who had just pulled his SUV around for Scarlett. He'd stopped the vehicle at the curb.

"What?" She certainly hadn't expected that question from him. "Of course, I feel safe with Grant."

A faint line appeared between her lawyer's brows. "The man has quite a reputation."

She wasn't sure what that meant.

"And Justin Turner seemed to think Grant could be the man responsible for those attacks."

She laughed. The sound held no humor. "Justin also thought I was responsible. He's drinking too much. Looking to blame someone for what happened to his brother." Scarlett shook her head. "But Grant isn't the killer."

She started to walk down the last few steps.

"But he is *a* killer."

Scarlett paused and looked back at Pierce.

"I can see it in his eyes," her lawyer said softly. "It's a look I've encountered before, with other clients." He closed the distance between them. "That look tells me that they've crossed the line. Given in to the dark."

She tilted her head. "You never asked me if I was innocent or guilty." She'd actually been surprised that he'd agreed to take her case. He'd been Eric's friend, not hers, but when she'd called him from jail, he'd agreed to represent her.

"I never ask any of my clients that. I can't, and I don't want to know." His eyes had returned to Grant once more. "My job is to represent my clients, not to judge them." He cleared his throat. "But you're different. One look in your eyes, and I knew." He slid her his card.

"I already have—"

"My personal number is on the back. If you should feel frightened, or if you think that being in Grant Mc-Guire's company isn't the safest bet, call me." His fingers curled around hers. "You got away once. What if you don't again?"

The card was crisp in her grasp. There was worry in Pierce's eyes.

"Scarlett?"

She turned at Grant's call. Her lawyer let her go.

As she hurried toward Grant, Scarlett tucked the card into her pocket. He wasn't a threat to her. Pierce was wrong. He didn't know Grant like she did.

Grant was a man she could trust. She'd always known that.

She slid into the SUV.

Grant shut the door behind her.

PIERCE WATCHED SCARLETT drive away. She'd thought he was wrong to worry. She trusted Grant McGuire far too much.

Pierce trusted no one. After all he'd seen and done in his business, no, you *couldn't* trust anyone.

The SUV's taillights disappeared.

He turned and made his way back into the police

station. As usual, the place was buzzing with activity. Always was. Crime never stopped.

That's why my business is booming.

But some days, he sure hated his business.

Detective Shayne Townsend was hunched over his desk. Pierce approached him and tapped him lightly on his shoulder. "A moment of your time, Detective."

Shayne frowned at him. "You just had more than a few moments. Your client is gone now."

"Um, she is. But it's not Scarlett that I want to discuss."

He saw the detective's flash of surprise.

"It's Grant McGuire."

Chapter Seven

"The ranch?" Surprise raised Scarlett's voice as they pulled toward the long, winding drive that would take them to the McGuire ranch. "What are we doing here?"

She'd fallen asleep shortly after they'd left the police station. After the hell of her previous night, Grant had known that Scarlett needed her rest. So he'd driven... and he'd found himself going not to his house, but to the family ranch.

He didn't go there often. Too many memories were in that place. Some good. Some bad. Some so painful he could never forget them.

I lost my parents here.

And he'd also lost Scarlett there. Back on the little bluff that overlooked the lake.

"You need to be able to relax for a bit. Not worry about reporters dodging your steps." He inclined his head toward the ranch. "No one will bother you here."

And the security at the ranch was top-notch. After their parents' murder, he and his brothers had made sure that the place was as secure as Fort Knox.

At first, the family had thought about selling the ranch. But Davis and Brodie had raged against that. The twins had been determined to keep the ranch, and they'd fought tooth and nail to get what they wanted.

The SUV drove slowly along that winding path.

"I don't come here much," he confessed. Because remembering the good times hurt. Thinking about what he'd lost.

Scarlett's fingertips brushed over his arm.

I lost too much.

He braked the SUV near the main house and turned to look at her. Her worried stare was on the entrance. She was biting her lip.

His hand lifted and he tapped that lip.

Her breath rushed out, tickling over his skin, and he let his finger linger against her mouth.

If she only knew the things I want to do to her.

He slowly lowered his hand. "You can go inside and sleep, if you want. No one will bother you." He'd make sure of it. "Or you can ride. I'll saddle up a horse for you." He gave her a weak smile.

She shook her head. "I've never been very good at horseback riding. Not like you."

He thought she'd been pretty damn good. When she'd ridden across the land with her hair streaming behind her, she'd always taken his breath away.

"I think I'll just go for a walk," Scarlett said. She turned from him and opened the door.

And Grant followed suit.

He wasn't particularly surprised to see the twins stride onto the porch. Brodie appeared first. Tall, fit, with hair that he kept cropped a little too short, Brodie grinned when he saw Grant. The grin flashed his dimples.

"It's about time you came out here, brother," Brodie said.

The porch creaked as Davis appeared behind his twin. The two were identical, except Davis had longer hair, and his dimples never flashed.

Davis had a rule about smiling.

He'd rather glare at the world.

Both had been Navy SEALs, and both were absolutely lethal in combat.

"Though I didn't expect to be seeing you with such lovely company," Brodie added as he turned his killer smile toward Scarlett.

Brodie had never met a woman that he thought he couldn't charm. He didn't seem to be happy unless he was hooking up with a new lady, though his hookups rarely lasted long.

One month was currently his time limit.

"Hello, Brodie." Scarlett's voice was soft. "Davis. It's been a while."

Brodie hopped off the porch step and hugged her. "Too long."

The twins had always liked Scarlett. Well, Brodie had, anyway. As for Davis…

Davis took his time climbing off the steps. He caught Brodie's shoulder and pulled him back. "Give the woman some breathing space," he ordered.

But then he brought Scarlett in for a big bear hug.

"You don't have to be scared," Grant heard Davis tell her. "We won't let anything happen to you."

Davis always thought I was a fool for leaving Scarlett behind.

Davis had an annoying habit about being right, about nearly everything.

Scarlett squeezed him back, then eased away. Her gaze flickered toward the ranch house. Sadness shadowed her face, but the emotion quickly vanished.

Grant understood. He felt the same sadness. His parents had been murdered inside the house. He didn't understand how Davis and Brodie could want to stick around that place.

He cleared his throat. "Scarlett wanted to take a walk."

Brodie's brows climbed. "Still can't ride a horse, huh, Scarlett?" Then he slapped Davis's arm. "That's okay. Neither can he."

Scarlett shook her head. "You still give your brother a hard time?"

"Only every minute."

And it was true. Brodie loved to rib his twin. Davis never mocked him back. He just sighed.

A lot.

"Are you two…you're both doing well?" Scarlett asked carefully.

"We're working on your case," Davis told her. "We'll be doing better when we find the killer out there."

And they *would* find him.

"I'll be doing better then, too." Scarlett sent them a quick smile, then turned and started making her way toward the bluff.

Grant watched her go.

Silence fell on the group. Then, as soon as Scarlett was out of earshot, Davis said softly, "She looks more delicate than I remember."

"Fear can do that." The humor was gone from Brodie's face, and when Grant glanced at him, there was no sign of his dimples. "It can break you."

"She's strong." Grant's eyes returned to her slender figure. "She's a survivor."

"Does she know?" Brodie asked, his voice curious.

"Know what?" Grant's eyes were still on her. Was she really heading to their old spot? He went there whenever he could force himself to come out to the ranch.

He'd gone to the ranch today only because he thought

it was the one place reporters wouldn't attack. They *couldn't* attack it. Not with the giant gate in the front and all their enhanced security around the exterior.

"Know that you love her, of course." Brodie spoke as if that were obvious. "I mean, you're staring after her like some kind of mooning teenager."

Grant's gaze snapped toward him. Younger brothers were such a pain in the—

"I read in the paper," Davis said, speaking before Grant could do more than growl at Brodie, "about the baby. Was that true or just some tabloid gossip to sell more issues?"

Grant shifted his stare back toward the bluff. He couldn't see Scarlett. "It was true."

Davis exhaled. "I'm sorry."

So was he. Sorrier than he could say. *Things will be different this time.* They had to be. He cleared his throat. "What have you found out on Eric Turner?"

"We finished going through his financials. Nothing too unusual." Now Davis was striding closer to Grant. "Other than the fact that he gave his younger brother twenty grand every month."

Grant's eyes widened and he gave a low whistle. "Twenty grand?"

"Like clockwork. The first of the month came around and, bam, a check was sent."

"Why?" Grant rounded on his brother. He'd thought Justin Turner had a steady job—

"Because the guy was demoted at his law firm about six months ago. Seems he had a drinking problem, and his big brother was trying to help him out." Davis ran a hand over his chin. "But one of Justin's coworkers overheard them fighting a few weeks back. Eric was telling him that the cash wouldn't keep coming."

"I'm guessing he didn't respond well to that." Just how angry had Justin been? "Now that Eric's dead, what happens to his estate?"

It was Brodie who answered. "Their parents are dead. Both passed from natural causes a few years back. And since he and Scarlett didn't marry, his estate will revert to Justin."

"No more cash problems," Davis murmured.

No. And Grant knew that plenty of people would kill—and *had* killed—for money. "We need eyes on him."

"Sullivan is already taking care of that."

Grant nodded.

"And Mac is on his way to track down Ian Lake."

Mac…that would be their brother Mackenzie. Just hearing Ian's name had caused Grant to clench his fists.

"Got some conflicting reports on the guy, so Mac wanted to do some hands-on reconnaissance."

That news put Grant on edge. "What conflicting reports?"

"Seems the guy might be dead… Hard to say for sure because despite a death certificate, the guy's credit cards were used just two months ago."

Hell. The case kept getting more tangled. Grant found himself peering over at the bluff once more, looking for Scarlett.

Brodie sighed. "Again? You can't seem to keep your eyes off her."

He ignored that because he'd just caught sight of Scarlett. Her hair was blowing in the light breeze.

"He's got it bad again," Davis announced. "Maybe one of us should take over guard duty, Grant. Let you get a little…distance here."

"No." It was an immediate denial.

"And why's that?" Davis asked, sounding a bit insulted. "I think Brodie and I are more than up to the task of guarding Scarlett."

Sure they were, but… "She feels comfortable with me. You two guys would just put her on edge."

Total lie.

"Well, we also wouldn't try to get her in bed." Brodie's voice was mild. Amused. "But something tells me that's high on your to-do list."

Grant glared at him.

"Take some advice…" Brodie offered.

Was he serious? Romance advice? From Mr. Love 'Em and Leave 'Em? Grant shook his head. This had to be good. Or bad. Very, very bad.

"Maybe this time you should actually let the woman know how you feel instead of, you know, pulling a Grant and going radio silent on her."

Pulling a Grant?

His eyes narrowed to near slits. "Thanks, Brodie. I'll be sure to remember that helpful tip." He rolled back his shoulders. He knew that Scarlett wanted her space, and she should be safe out there, walking along the bluff.

But he wanted to be with her. He even took a step that way, then stopped.

He wasn't going to cage Scarlett. He wanted to protect her, not trap her.

Exhaling slowly, he turned away and faced the ranch house. He hated this place, hated that house that always made him see blood and lost happiness. The bodies had been gone by the time he'd made it back to the US, but blood had stained the floor. And after all his battles, it had been too easy to image the sight of the dead in there. "We should have sold this place," he said.

Ava hadn't been back to the house, not since that night.

He didn't blame her.

"This land has been in our family for almost one hundred years." Davis's voice was low. "It *will* see joy again." He had been the one who'd fought the hardest to keep the place.

And Brodie... Well, when his twin wanted something badly enough, Brodie would always back him.

"Fine," Grant growled. That was pretty much the way he'd given in before, when they'd all sat in the lawyer's office, faces grim, as they'd tried to decide what in the hell to do next.

"But I think it's time to tear this house down. Keep the land, but build something new." Something that didn't remind them all too much of their past.

And of the nightmare that still hadn't ended.

Why were they being targeted? Who did it?

No evidence, not so much as a fingerprint, had been left behind. No motive. No suspects.

But we will find you...we will.

He didn't follow Scarlett onto the bluff and he didn't head into the house that still made his heart ache. Instead, he turned and marched toward the stables. He was in the mood for a ride. Wild and hard. Maybe if he rode fast enough, he'd even be able to escape from the ghosts of his past.

SCARLETT DIDN'T KNOW how long she stood on the bluff. The breeze was light against her face, easing the heat of the Texas sun.

She remembered coming there so often when she'd been a teen. She'd sneak onto the land to watch Grant. He'd worked so much with the horses. Whenever he'd come back from his tours of duty, he'd always ridden first thing. Ridden so fast that he'd almost scared her.

It had seemed as if he were running from demons.

She wondered…had any of those demons ever caught up to him?

She headed back toward the ranch house when the sun started to dip in the sky. She'd hidden long enough. Gotten control of herself and was now ready to face the world again. She had just caught sight of the house when she heard the pounding of a horse's hooves. Glancing to the right, she saw a big black horse racing toward the stable. Dirt flew up in its wake. And, his body angled low on that horse, a wide devil-may-care grin on his lips, Grant held tight to the animal.

Scarlett stopped walking. The past and present merged for her as she stared at Grant. When she'd seen him ride before, she'd always thought he looked so powerful. So strong.

Unstoppable.

She'd viewed him as perfect once. Too perfect. That image had shattered, and now she saw him for what he was.

Dangerous. Deadly.

Not some childhood hero. Not the white knight.

Something more.

He reined in the horse. She still hadn't moved.

He jumped off, and his hands ran over the animal's coat as he talked softly, soothingly. She kept watching as Grant cooled down his mount and took it inside.

Scarlett shivered a bit as she stood there. Grant had disappeared into the stables, and she could see the lights shining from inside. She took a few steps in that direction, and Grant appeared again. He saw her, and this time he was the one who froze.

There was sweat on his face. He had old gloves on his hands. His T-shirt molded around his rippled muscles and his jeans were covered with a layer of dust. He had been riding hell-bent, she knew. She shouldn't have found him sexy. Not when he looked so rough and wicked, but maybe that was why he looked so seductive right then.

There was nothing controlled about Grant in that moment.

She liked it.

Scarlett was tired of control. Tired of watching her every word and her every step.

He pulled off his gloves, put them on the top of a fence post and headed toward her with slow steps. His gaze raked over her. "You all right?"

She wanted him to stop doing that. To stop looking at her as if she was a victim. There was more to her than just the mess that was happening to her life right then.

She'd been on that bluff, and instead of thinking about the man after her, Scarlett's mind had kept wandering back to Grant. Remembering him.

Remembering the first time they'd been together. She'd been so nervous. So excited.

He'd been patient. Tender.

Even though she'd felt the fierce tension in his muscles, she'd known he was fighting desperately to hold on to his control. For her.

"Scarlett?" Worry flickered over his face.

Her hand lifted toward him. "Will you walk with me?"

He didn't take it. "Let me shower. I'm a mess. I should—"

"Walk with me," she said again, because she just wanted to be with him then.

His brow furrowed, as if he couldn't quite figure her out, but he took her hand.

They headed back toward the bluff. Lights shone

from within the ranch house, but she noticed Grant never looked that way.

"It's hard for you," Scarlett whispered, "being back here."

He nodded. His fingers tightened around hers.

"Then why are we here?"

"Because I thought you'd…because no one would be watching you here. You could take a few hours to relax."

That was exactly what she'd done. For a bit, she'd stopped feeling like a bug under a microscope. But it had hurt him to be there. "I'm sorry," she told him.

He glanced toward her. He had stubble lining his jaw. She wanted to press her fingers to that hard jaw, but she didn't. Did he know how much she loved his jaw? Perfectly square, strong.

"What do you have to be sorry for?"

"You shouldn't have to face this place, and the pain here, for me."

"Oh, Scarlett…" Her name was a sigh. "Don't you realize I'd face just about anything for you?"

Those words had her tensing, but she kept walking. Soon they were on the bluff, beneath the trees, staring out at the small lake. The area was so beautiful.

"I remember, you know." His voice was low. And his thumb was lightly rubbing her inner wrist. "What it was like the first time, here, with you."

She'd never been able to forget.

"I kept telling myself…go slow. *Go slow.*" His eyes were on the lake. "But really, all I wanted to do was rip away that little dress you had on and get inside of you as fast as I could."

Her breath was coming a bit too quickly.

"I knew you were a virgin." He was still gazing at the lake, but she wondered if she was actually seeing it. "And

I wanted to show you that I could be more than some clumsy soldier. That I could take care of you."

"I never thought you were a clumsy soldier."

He glanced at her. "What did you think of me?"

The question caught her off guard.

."I mean, hell, I know why I was so obsessed with you back then."

Obsessed? She'd never thought of it that way.

"I saw you in the hallway at school. The light was hitting your hair, and the way you looked…it was like you were some kind of angel." He lifted his hand. His fingers hovered above her lips, but he didn't touch her. "Yet you had a mouth that made me think of sin."

Her heartbeat was drumming fast and hard in her chest.

"I played the gentleman with you for so long."

She'd always sensed his restraint.

His hand fell back to his side. "You never got to see how I really was. I was too afraid of scaring you away."

"You don't scare me, Grant," she told him. He hadn't ten years ago. He didn't now.

"Maybe I *should* scare you." He paced away from her. "Because that obsession? I don't think it's gone."

"Grant…"

"It's worse now." He'd turned his back on her. "I see you, and I think that there's no reason for me to hold back anymore. We're adults. Single. Free." He glanced over at her. "And I know just how good we are together. So damn good."

She had to swallow the lump that had risen in her throat. They *were* good together.

"But I'm done pretending to be someone else. I'm not the gentleman." He turned fully toward her. The setting sun was behind him, casting shadows on the ground. "I never will be."

His hands were at his sides, his legs braced apart.

"I'm an ex-soldier who learned too many ways to kill."

Why was he telling her this?

"I spent years in battle zones, spent years learning to be as lethal as I could be."

He took a step toward her. She refused to retreat.

"So when people warn you about me—they're right. I do have a reputation."

Had he heard Pierce's words to her at the police station?

"I'm dangerous, but only to my enemies. I'm single-minded in my determination. I don't always fight fair, and I more than know how to get my hands dirty."

He advanced another step. Her spine straightened as she stared at him.

"I want you," he said flatly. His lips twisted, but that smile didn't reach his eyes. "Someone close said I should tell you how I feel, so I will. *I want you.* Every minute. I dreamed about getting you back in my bed for years, but those were just dreams."

Dreams she'd had, too.

"Now that you're back in my life, now that I had you again, it's worse, Scarlett. So much worse." He did touch her then. His hand lifted and he pushed back the hair that had blown across her cheek. "Because all I can think about when I get close to you…"

He was so close.

"…is having you naked beneath me again."

She licked her lips. His gaze immediately fell to her mouth.

"That's how I feel." His voice was gravel rough. "Like

I'd do anything to have you again. Because I need you, more than I've ever needed any other woman."

Her hands rose and curled around his shoulders. "Are you going to ask me how I feel?" Her voice was soft, when his had been so hard.

"How do you feel?"

"I've dreamed about you, for years. Sometimes I'd wake from those dreams, and I'd hate you."

He flinched.

But she wasn't going to lie. Scarlett wouldn't pretend with him. He'd left, and when he had, he'd ripped out her heart.

She'd never really let anyone else get close to her after him. And Eric had tried.

"And sometimes," she said, "I'd wake up, and I'd miss you so much."

His fingers curled around her jaw.

"I remember our first time, too. It was right here, under the stars. You brought a blanket for us, and we'd had a picnic out here." He'd come back from battle then, another mission that had started to leave the darkness in his eyes. "You were different that night." Less the perfect suitor—the gentleman role he played—and more a man who'd touched her with heated desire. "I didn't want you to go slow. I just wanted you."

"Scarlett…" Her name was a desperate growl. Sensual tension thickened the air between them.

"I'm not looking for the man you were back then. The girl I was ten years ago, she's gone, too." No one stayed the same after that length of time. "Your darkness—I can see it, Grant." *I could always see it.* "And I'm not scared of it."

No matter how many warnings he gave her, she wouldn't be afraid. She trusted Grant.

"I want you," she told him softly. And it was true. Facing death sure had a way of making things crystal clear.

Life wasn't about hesitation. It was about taking what you wanted. Enjoying the moment while you had it.

So Scarlett didn't wait for Grant to lean down and kiss her. She rose onto her toes and pressed her mouth to his.

I want you.

Chapter Eight

The past and present twisted for Grant as he tasted Scarlett. Her mouth was so soft beneath his. Those lips made for sin were tempting him, pushing him to the edge of reason.

He'd warned her. She hadn't listened. His desire for her wasn't something that he could control.

It wasn't something he wanted to control.

He backed her under the protective branches of the tree that waited nearby. Once upon a time, he'd even carved their initials into that tree.

A lifetime ago.

When he'd thought they might have forever, and then he'd realized…

She doesn't belong with someone like me.

Because Scarlett was good. Sweet. She didn't understand the evil that he faced. All too often, he wondered… was that evil in him, too?

He'd done things, so many things, that he never wanted to tell her about. Because Scarlett had looked at him with light in her eyes, and he'd never wanted that light to vanish.

His mouth grew harder on hers when he heard the faint moan slip from her lips. He loved that little moan.

Her dress blew around them, and the past rose up once more.

Only this time, she wasn't a virgin.

And he didn't have to be the gentleman.

"Scarlett." If they didn't stop in the next minute, there would be no stopping at all for him.

Her hips pressed against him. She had to feel the heavy ridge of his desire. For her. Always *her*.

She licked his lower lip, a sensual swipe of her tongue that had him shuddering.

No one can see us here. I can have her.

His hand slid down. He lifted the skirt and touched the silk of her leg. Higher, higher his hand rose, and then he felt the softness of her panties.

He stroked her through the lace, loving the way she felt against his hand. Warm and eager, she arched toward him.

He wanted to thrust as deep into her as he could go.

This had been their place. He'd been his happiest in that spot by the lake, with her.

He kissed her again, long and hard, even as his fingers kept stroking. Her body grew tense against him, and her breath came faster.

"I don't…have protection…" He'd been so intent on getting her to the ranch that he hadn't even thought—

"I'm on the pill. I'm…clean." Her fingers had slid down his chest.

His eyes widened as he stared at her. She was telling him that he could take her, flesh to flesh.

"I'm clean, too," he whispered back.

Her lips lifted in the faintest of smiles. The waning sunlight fell on them.

An angel…

She should have stayed far away from him. The obsession truly was just growing stronger.

He lifted her up, holding her easily, and making sure that he didn't touch her bandage. He lifted her up—

And he yanked those panties out of the way. They dropped to the ground, and now that he could touch her fully, he parted her folds and sank into her.

Her skirt fluttered around them. He'd unhooked his jeans, but was still dressed.

But he had her.

He was *in* her. And it felt like heaven.

In and out, he thrust. Her legs wrapped tightly around his hips and her nails dug into his shoulders. She pushed her body against his, and he drove as deeply into her as he could go.

There was no restraint. No seduction.

There was only need. Only pleasure. Desire spinning out of control as he thrust harder. As he took more and more...

And Scarlett was with him every step of the way. She shuddered in his arms. She called out his name, and Grant felt the ripple of her release all around him.

He followed her. Seemed to erupt inside her as the pleasure exploded within him, through him. He held her as tightly as he could, and the thunder of his heartbeat filled his ears.

WHERE WAS SHE?

Scarlett hadn't gone back to her condo, and Grant McGuire's home was dark. There was no vehicle in McGuire's drive. Nothing to indicate they'd been there in hours.

Had he taken Scarlett to a hotel? Some out-of-the-way spot so that they could vanish for a while?

Scarlett doesn't get to vanish. She gets to suffer.

He glared at Grant's house. They had to come back. Sooner or later. Scarlett would have to return for court. She'd have to come back to face the charges against her. It wasn't over. She didn't just get to ride off into the sunset.

But…

He smiled as he stared at the house.

But this was an opportunity for him. The perfect time to start laying his trap.

And under the cover of the darkness, he made his way to Grant McGuire's house.

NIGHT HAD FALLEN. When Scarlett tipped back her head, she could see the stars starting to peek out. She was still in Grant's arms, still held tightly and she didn't want to move.

If she did, she'd have to go back to reality. She didn't want to, not yet.

But Grant was stirring. "Did I…hurt you?"

She wished he wouldn't worry about that. She wasn't some delicate doll that would shatter if he held her too hard. She was a flesh-and-blood woman, and she'd wanted him.

All of him.

"Your wound… I tried to be—"

She kissed his jaw. That sexy stubble. "I'm fine."

He eased her to her feet. Those feet definitely weren't too stable right then, but his hands were on her, holding her steady when she would have staggered. Then he slowly slid her panties back up her legs. She felt his head turn, and he pressed a kiss to her inner thigh. It was a tender caress, and it caught her off guard. Why, she didn't know. He'd been tender plenty of times before.

But he said that was a role…

"I can't get enough of you." His dark confession. But it could have been hers, because already, Scarlett wanted more. As he rose, his fingers tangled with her own. "That took the edge off," Grant said, "for now. But I want more, Scarlett, so much more."

So did she.

She wanted everything he had to give.

In silence, they walked back to the SUV. Their steps were steady as they covered the distance. A few moments later, her gaze slid toward the main house. The front door was shut. Brodie was near the stables; she could see him and—

"Leaving so soon?" Davis's voice came from the shadows, and Scarlett jumped.

"Sorry. Didn't mean to scare you." He stepped forward, cocking his head as he glanced at Grant. "Maybe you should spend the night out here."

But Grant shook his head. "No, we need to—"

His phone rang then, the quick peal loud and sharp. She hadn't even realized that he'd even had that phone with him. But her mind *had* been on other things.

He pulled out his phone. "Sullivan, what is it?"

Her body tensed. With the way things had been going, Scarlett expected more bad news. She expected—

"My house? *What. The. Hell?* Yeah, yeah, I'm on my way right now." He shoved the phone into his back pocket. Even in the darkness, his sudden intense ferocity was palpable. "Sullivan is at my place—and my house is on fire."

"What?" Shock roughened Davis's voice.

But Grant was already running for his SUV. And, not about to be left, Scarlett jumped in with him.

When they raced away from the ranch, Davis and Brodie were following right behind them.

FIREFIGHTERS WERE ON the scene when Grant braked to a stop in front of his house. The flames shot toward the sky, billowing up into the darkness.

Rage poured through him, just as hot as the fire that was destroying his home. He jumped from his SUV and stormed forward. Sullivan was already there. He turned toward Grant, his face tense. "I'm sorry. I came by because I wanted to leave some intel on Louis East. I saw the flames." He gave a sad shake of his head. "It was already burning too hot by then for me to control the blaze."

Grant had no close neighbors. So no one would have seen the fire. If Sullivan hadn't come by—hell, it was too late, no matter what.

The roof gave a loud groan. Shuddered. A section at the upper right began to cave in.

He felt a light touch on his arm. He turned, and Scarlett was there. Her gaze was on the fire.

"Oh, Grant…" Sympathy, pain, cracked in those words. "It's—"

Gone.

The windows in the front of his house exploded.

MEN WHO WERE with Scarlett Stone…those were men who lost everything that mattered to them. Grant McGuire was learning that lesson right now.

He watched from the shadows as the firefighters tried to control the flames. Only there was no stopping the inferno. He'd been too careful when he'd started that fire. Some tips from a serial arsonist…oh, he'd learned very well.

The accelerant had been perfect. The timing. The eruption of those flames…

And Grant got to watch his home burn to ash. How perfect.

Scarlett was there, holding tightly to the man staring

sadly up at the house. Did she realize what was happening? That it was all her fault? Probably not. She thought she was the victim.

She was the perpetrator.

But at least the fire had served its purpose. Two purposes, really.

To punish Grant McGuire.

And to bring Scarlett out of hiding. Now, he had her in his sights.

He wouldn't lose her again.

THE FLAMES WERE TWISTING, snaking ever higher into the sky. Grant's body was like stone as he watched his home go up in flames.

A fire shouldn't consume, not so quickly, so fully.

"It was set." Sullivan sounded certain.

Scarlett feared the same thing. She glanced over and saw that Grant's brother's gaze was on her.

"Good thing you two weren't here," he added. "Houses can be replaced. People can't." His hand settled on Grant's shoulder. "I'm sorry," he said again.

Grant nodded, but he wasn't staring at the house with sorrow on his face. He was glaring with fury, and his hands were tightly clenched fists at his sides.

Scarlett figured it was only a matter of time until Detective Townsend showed up. She turned away from the blaze, and her gaze swept the area around the burning house. Most of the surroundings were in darkness, but—

Something glinted in the dark.

"Grant." Her voice was a bare whisper. Maybe she'd imagined that glint.

Then she saw it again.

At her whisper, Grant had turned toward her.

"I think someone is watching us." No, she didn't just *think* it. She was *certain* that someone was out there.

Grant swore, and she knew that he'd caught sight of that little glint. A reflection of the light off something.

Some*one*.

"Sullivan." Grant's voice snapped with command.

"Already on it." His brother was moving fast.

So was Grant.

Scarlett scrambled to keep up with them.

THEY'D SEEN HIM.

He jumped back, grabbing for his phone and the binoculars. His truck waited nearby, the accelerants still in the back. Or what was left of them.

The McGuires were running toward his hiding spot, and he cranked the truck's engine as fast as he could. Now wasn't the time for them to catch him. He was supposed to be watching them, not the other way around.

I'm not the one you hunt.

He was supposed to stay, supposed to watch Scarlett.

But they were nearly on top of him. He slammed his foot down on the gas pedal and the truck fishtailed as he lurched down a dirt road and away.

DUST SHOT INTO the air. The pickup truck heaved off with a roar of its engine.

The guy thought he was getting away? *Think again.* Grant yanked out his phone. "Davis…" He knew his brother was close. "Block the south-side perimeter of the property. Stop the pickup coming your way—stop him!"

Davis and Brodie would have only moments before that truck came barreling at them, but Grant knew they'd act fast. He spun back around and nearly ran into Scarlett.

He'd been so consumed by fury that he hadn't searched the scene. Scarlett had and because of her...*we've got this guy*.

He caught her hand and they ran back to his SUV, then jumped inside. Sullivan was already in his car, rushing away. Adrenaline pumped in Grant's blood as he floored his vehicle and gave chase.

Scarlett's hand slapped against the dashboard as they accelerated. He kept seeing the flames. *What if she'd been in that house? What if she'd been trapped in there?*

He drove even faster.

He swerved around the corner, following right behind Sullivan. *Faster, faster.*

Then he saw the makeshift roadblock up ahead. Brodie and Davis had covered that south side, all right. They'd blocked the narrow dirt road with their vehicle. And they were both standing outside of it, their guns pointed at the truck, which had just come to a jarring halt.

Grant slammed on his brakes, too.

Up ahead, Sullivan jumped out of his car.

"Stay here," Grant told Scarlett, and he grabbed his gun from the glove compartment.

"You're kidding, right?" She leaped out of the SUV. "Not after what he's done!"

Grant rushed around the vehicle, grabbed her and put her behind him. Did the woman even realize she wasn't armed? Fury was fine, but it wouldn't stop a man ready to attack with a gun.

The truck's interior was dark. The guy inside hadn't moved.

"Call Detective Townsend," Grant told Scarlett. Then he raised his voice and shouted, "Come out!" He kept his weapon aimed at the vehicle.

There was no escape for the man inside. Sullivan had

taken up a position near the driver's side door, his weapon pointed. Davis and Brodie were in cover position, too, and Grant suspected they were just looking for a reason to attack.

"Come out," he shouted again. "Come out or—"

The door opened, and the squeak of it seemed so loud in the darkness.

The fire was still burning. The scent stung Grant's nose and had his jaw clenching. "Put your hands up!" he ordered. "Get out now."

Behind him, Grant heard Scarlett talking on the phone to Detective Townsend. He was sure Shayne would burn rubber getting out here.

As for the man in that truck...

His hands appeared first. Shaking. First the left hand, then the right, showing that he wasn't armed.

None of the McGuires relaxed their positions. Not even for a second.

Then the guy's foot appeared, some fancy, ridiculous shoe.

"Step away from the truck," Grant ordered, "then turn and face me."

Slowly, the man complied. He inched away from the truck and turned...

"Justin?" Scarlett's voice was stunned.

His head jerked toward her.

And that was when Grant saw the gun, tucked into Justin Turner's belt.

"Get back, Scarlett," Grant told her. "Get back to the SUV."

She started inching back.

And Justin began to advance.

"Stop!" Grant barked at him. "Don't take another step!"

The man didn't stop. "I'm going to lose it all, lose everything now."

Sullivan was creeping toward him.

"Yeah, well, maybe you should have thought of that before you torched my house." Grant could even see the empty gas cans in the back of the truck. "Now freeze or I will shoot you."

Justin stopped. He wasn't looking at Grant, but at Scarlett as she slid back. "You told my brother to cut me off," he accused.

"No, no, I didn't—"

"How was I supposed to live, if he wasn't helping? And I just needed the help a little while longer." His hand dropped and rubbed against his leg, far too close to that gun for Grant's peace of mind.

"Sullivan." Grant's voice ripped with warning. This wasn't going well. They needed to get that weapon away from the guy.

"But Eric wasn't helping anymore. Because of you." Justin's tone became harder. "He wanted to make you happy. To do anything for you, and you didn't even love him!"

Scarlett had stilled, and that was actually good. Because Grant was afraid that if she ran, Justin would reach for his gun.

"I never told him anything about you," she said, her voice soft. "Never. I don't know what you're talking about!"

"I'm losing everything! No job, no house…all my debts are being called in. I'm done, because of you and Eric! Freaking perfect Eric!"

Sirens wailed in the distance.

At the sound, Justin's hand flew up and he grabbed the gun from his belt. He yanked it out and aimed—

At Scarlett.

Grant didn't hesitate. His finger squeezed the trigger of his own weapon and he fired.

His bullet hit its mark as Justin stumbled—and just as another bullet blasted into him.

The second hit had Justin falling to his knees.

Chapter Nine

"Sometimes a man loses his grasp on sanity, and he goes too far…" Detective Townsend turned his head and watched as Justin Turner was loaded into the back of an ambulance. "Or at least, that's probably the spin his lawyer will give on what went down here tonight." Bitterness entered his voice. "Won't be the first time I've seen an insanity plea. Won't be the last, either."

Scarlett rubbed her arms. The cops had swarmed in, but they hadn't appeared soon enough. Grant had shot Justin, and Sullivan had fired seconds later. Grant's bullet had sank into the man's right shoulder, and Sully's had slammed into his side.

Neither shot had been fatal. Justin would live to stand trial.

Like I almost did.

"All the accelerants are right there," Shayne said as he inclined his head toward the abandoned truck. "Guess he thought he could get away clean from the scene and then destroy all the evidence of his crime."

"He thought wrong," Grant said grimly.

Grant had been too controlled, too quiet, since the shooting. His emotions were on lockdown, Scarlett could tell, and she kept casting nervous glances his way.

"I'm sending men to Turner's house now. They'll do

a thorough search. There could be more evidence there for us to use—"

"Do you think he killed Eric?" Scarlett asked. She kept replaying Justin's last words to her. Money...yes, money could definitely be a motive for murder.

"He was the one who kept pushing so hard for your prosecution," Shayne said. He exhaled a rough sigh. "Called the captain every day. Was always talking to the reporters, and now with this mess tonight..." The detective's words trailed away. "Let's just see what we find." He hesitated. "But if I were a betting man, I'd say we have our killer."

The clench in her gut told Scarlett he was right. All the pieces in this twisted puzzle were finally falling into place. She looked to the left, her gaze helplessly returning to Grant. His eyes were on the ambulance.

"A guard will stay with him?" he demanded.

"At all times," Shayne assured him.

Scarlett's shoulders slumped. "It's over."

Grant's head turned toward her.

"He practically confessed, Grant," she whispered. "Right in front of us all." The scent of ash drifted into the air. *His house.* "We're safe now. It's over."

But Grant shook his head.

She reached out to him. It was strange. He was right in front of her, but it felt as if he were a thousand miles away. Even when she touched him, Scarlett still had the strange feeling that he wasn't there. Not really. "Grant?" Concern laced her voice.

"I'll want to talk with him," Grant said flatly, his attention back on Justin and that ambulance. "As soon as he's awake."

Because Justin hadn't been conscious when he'd been

loaded into the ambulance. The EMTs had been working on him, but he'd been out cold.

"After I get my crack at him," Shayne said, "I'll see what I can do." He inclined his head toward them. "I'll need statements from you both. We'll get the preliminaries down tonight then you can come by the station tomorrow for follow-up."

The station…her home away from home.

Grant's home is gone.

When Shayne walked away, Scarlett tightened her hold on Grant. "I'm so sorry about your house."

He shook his head. "Bricks and wood. It didn't matter." His eyes seemed to blaze—a green fire. "You matter." Then his hands were up and holding tight to her. "He was going to shoot you, you know that? Kill you. Right in front of me."

She would never forget the moment when that gun had turned on her.

"What the hell would I have done then?" Grant demanded.

Before she could answer, one of the cops called out to him. Time for his statement. Right. With a curse, Grant pulled from her. Scarlett stood there, chill bumps rising on her arms.

Then she felt a whisper of air against her, a slight rustle. She turned, and Davis was at her side.

Davis had always been able to move so silently, like a predator, long before he'd honed his skills as a SEAL.

"That was too close," he murmured, his voice pitched low, to carry only to her ears.

"I didn't expect him to have a gun." Eric had been attacked with a knife. So had Louis. And when the killer broke into her place, he'd been armed with a knife then, too. *Never a gun.*

"Always expect people to go out fighting. The instinct for survival is too strong."

She glanced back over at Grant. She had to do it. It just seemed as if she needed to watch him. *Why do I feel like he's pulling away from me?*

"But I wasn't talking about that jerk pulling his weapon. I was talking about just how close Grant came to killing him."

Her chill bumps got worse.

"Grant is a damn fine shot. One of the best I've ever seen."

Scarlett tried to take slow, deep breaths.

"In a situation like that...we've all been trained to respond instinctively. If someone is pointing a gun at you, you stop that perp. You take him out."

She couldn't take her eyes off Grant. "Grant shot him in the shoulder," she whispered.

"Only because Justin tripped at the last second."

And she remembered the way he had stumbled. A little stagger that had hunched and twisted his body.

"Sometimes, men come to important realizations in this life. I'm guessing Grant just realized something very, very important."

She shook her head. She wasn't sure she wanted to hear more.

"He already realized he'd kill for his country. For his family. Now Grant knows that he'd kill for you, without any hesitation whatsoever."

Scarlett backed away from him.

"He was aiming for the guy's heart." Davis sounded absolutely certain.

"You can't know that."

"Sure I do. It's where I would have aimed, too." His head tilted as he studied her. "And now you know..."

She knew the world had gone crazy around her.

"...that man would kill to keep you safe." He paused. "And what would you do for him?"

Scarlett backed away from Davis's intense stare. She went straight to Grant and stared up at him.

But couldn't bring herself to ask...

Were you killing him, for me?

So she stood by his side—inches apart, but miles away.

THEY WENT BACK to the ranch. Grant was dead silent on the trip, and Scarlett didn't have any words to say, either. She was exhausted, physically and emotionally, and she just wanted to crash.

My home is still a crime scene. So going there hadn't been an option. And Grant's place was still smoldering.

So they'd followed the others back to the McGuire ranch.

But when they braked in front of the sprawling spread, Grant didn't move. He didn't turn off the engine. Didn't take his hands from the steering wheel.

"Grant?" She almost touched him, but there was a... coldness to him then. Her chill was already bad enough, so she flattened her hands on her lap.

Hours ago, we made love on that bluff. Now there was a stone wall between them.

It was easy enough for a killer to wreck happiness.

"We don't have to go inside," she rushed to say. She knew this place held too many ghosts for him. "We can go back and find a motel room someplace. We can—"

"The reporters will swarm when Justin's arrest hits the news. This is the best place for us." Finally, he killed the SUV's ignition. "We can stay in the guesthouse out back. We don't have to go in the main house."

Her breath left her in a relieved rush. Good. He wouldn't have to face off against the ghosts in there.

"Ava won't ever stay in the main house," Grant murmured. His fingers tightened around the steering wheel. "She can't go inside without shaking."

His pain was palpable, so despite the cold, Scarlett reached out and touched him.

He flinched. "You should be careful with me tonight."

Her hand stayed on his. "Why?"

"Because my control is gone." His head turned toward her. In the dark, he was a dangerous shadow. "He was going to kill you. Right in front of me. He was going to kill you!"

She unhooked her seat belt and leaned toward Grant. Her hands curled around his neck. "I'm fine. We're both fine. And he's not going to hurt us ever again." His muscles were harder than rock beneath her, and he wasn't holding her. She needed him to. Scarlett kissed his jaw. The stubble rasped over her lips. "We're safe now."

"Are you so sure?"

She pulled back, just enough to try and see his face. Faint light from the main house spilled into the SUV. She heard doors slamming.

Brodie and Davis.

She glanced out the windshield. The twins were heading into the house, giving her and Grant privacy.

"It's over," she said once more, as if saying it enough would make the words true. She *wanted* it to be over. "It's time for life to get back to normal." Scarlett slipped from his SUV. Once outside, she tipped back her head and stared up at the star-filled sky. Away from the bright lights of Austin, the sky was amazing. A million stars that went on forever.

Grant's door slammed, too. His footsteps crunched

over the dirt and gravel as he headed toward her. Slowly, her gaze slid away from the stars and toward the bluff. Had she really made love with him there, hours before? It seemed so long ago.

He caught her hand. Together, they headed for the guesthouse. Why did being with him feel so natural?

Easy.

But nothing in life was ever really easy.

He unlocked the door and led her inside. She flipped on the light and padded around the place, admiring the gleaming wooden table and chairs. The matching desk. The rocking chair. "Brodie's work, right?" Because she remembered the way he'd been as a teen. Always carving or working in his shop.

Grant shut the door. Leaned back against it. "Yes."

Her fingers trailed over the rocking chair. Brodie had always been gifted. She glanced up and found Grant's eyes on her. When she saw the heat in his stare, her fingers stilled, locking on the wood. "Grant?"

He stepped toward her. "I'm not usually scared."

She shook her head.

"I don't get scared in battle. I'm doing my job. My teammates count on me. There's no room for fear then."

Another step.

"I wasn't afraid when I learned about my parents' murder. I was furious."

She pulled in a desperate gulp of air. *His eyes...*

"But I was afraid tonight, when Justin tried to shoot you." Grant stopped in front of her. "I was afraid I'd lose you."

Scarlett stared up at him.

"I don't want to lose you. I lived without you for ten years. I don't want to lose you." Then he was reaching for her. One hand slid beneath the fall of her hair. The other caught her around the waist and pulled her against him.

He kissed her. Kissed her with a ferocious hunger and the wild desire that always seemed to be there, rushing between them.

Her hands flattened on his chest. She didn't even think of pushing him away. Why would she? Scarlett wanted him too much.

She rose onto her toes, opened her mouth and kissed him just as wildly. Grant wasn't the only one who'd been afraid. But when Justin had been reaching for that gun, Scarlett hadn't worried about her own life.

She'd worried about Grant.

She'd always feared for him. When they were dating, and he'd joined the military. When he'd disappeared into battles that he couldn't discuss. When he'd become a ranger and his eyes had grown so shadowed.

And now…when he hunted for killers as a PI. When he put his life on the line so often, she was afraid.

He was addicted to the rush of adrenaline. She'd learned that long ago.

Just as she'd learned to live with her fear. But tonight…tonight it had been too close for them both.

Her hands shoved his shirt up. She touched hot skin. He pulled back long enough to send that T-shirt flying, and then her hands were on the buckle of his belt. She managed to unsnap his jeans and then she dragged down his zipper.

There was no hesitancy from her. No uncertainty. This was Grant. He was what she wanted.

Life was short. Fate was cruel. And in this moment, there would be no regrets. No fears. There would be only need and pleasure.

They made it to the bed. She wasn't even really sure

how, because she'd been kissing him the whole time, but Scarlett felt the soft mattress against the back of her legs, and then they were tumbling down onto it.

They were still kissing.

Only now they were both fighting to get her clothes off. The dress—well, it was easy enough to ditch that.

Then he caught her underwear and slid it down her legs. She arched toward him, needing this moment so much.

Pleasure could hold back the fear. Pleasure could make the nightmares go away.

Her bra was tossed aside. Then his mouth was on her breast. Caressing. Kissing. Even as he kissed her, his fingers were sliding between her thighs, stroking her core. Making her arch up against him. Her breath came faster and harder as her body yearned for release.

"Grant...I don't want to wait."

She wanted him. Now. And she was taking what she wanted.

She pushed him onto his back, rose above him and straddled his strong hips.

Her knees sank into the mattress. Her fingers threaded with his. Scarlett kept her eyes locked with Grant's, and then she sank down, taking all of him into her.

He filled her fully, and a moan slipped from her. This was what she needed.

Up, down, her body moved. Her knees sank deeper into the mattress. His fingers tightened around hers.

She couldn't look away from his eyes.

Up and down...she could feel the approach of her climax, coiling within her, getting closer and closer.

She leaned forward and kissed him. Loved the way he licked her lower lip.

Her lips kept moving, her body arching.

The coil was tighter, tighter—

His hips pushed against her, driving deep, and the pleasure hit her. She was kissing him when she climaxed. Tasting him and wondering if he could taste her pleasure, too.

His hips thrust again. Over and over, and the pleasure rocked through her in waves that wouldn't end. Then he was growling her name, stiffening beneath her, and she knew the release had hit him, too.

Their hands were still linked. They were still kissing.

And, yes, she could taste his pleasure.

SCARLETT WAS ASLEEP in his arms, again.

She did that—just seemed to go right to sleep without any fears. Trusting that she was safe with him.

Moonlight flowed over them. She was beside him in the old bed, turned to face him. Her lashes cast shadows on her cheeks, and the curve of her shoulder looked both sensual and delicate.

He leaned forward and kissed that curve.

In her sleep, she murmured his name.

I won't lose you.

Scarlett thought the threats to her were over, that it was time to go back to her real life. Grant had every intention of being part of that real life.

He wasn't ready to be forgotten by Scarlett.

He wanted another chance with her. He'd do anything to get that chance. Anything.

Once more, his gaze returned to the window. In the distance, he could just see the roof of the main ranch house. He swallowed, pushing back the pain that wanted to rise within him. Life was filled with good and bad, he knew that.

He'd stayed away from this place because he couldn't stand the shadows of pain that clung to the ranch.

Brodie and Davis had stayed there because, when they looked around them, the twins just saw the good memories.

Grant bent and kissed Scarlett's shoulder once more. He wouldn't be leaving her in the middle of the night again. He wouldn't be running away. From now on, he intended to be at Scarlett's side.

He just had to convince her that she needed him there.

IT WAS THE faint scratch of wood that woke Grant hours later. He came awake instantly, the way he'd always done back in his military days. His eyes flew open, his heart pounded frantically in his chest, and he realized that Scarlett was still sleeping in his arms.

She slept deeply, easily.

But he could hear the creak of wood from the outer room. Starlight still filled the room, spilling in from the window. Dawn hadn't sent light streaking over the sky yet, and under the cover of darkness, someone had just sneaked into the guesthouse.

He slid from the bed. Brodie or Davis wouldn't just come in, not with Scarlett there. Could it be Sullivan? Or even Mac?

But, no, they didn't use the guesthouse.

Grant's steps were silent as he made his way toward the bedroom door. He could hear more faint creaks, and he knew his intruder was coming his way.

Grant yanked open the door and launched himself forward, a snarl on his lips and his hands ready to—

Grab his sister?

Because he recognized the desperate scream that had

just come from his intruder. It was one that had haunted him for far too long.

After he'd come back home, Ava had stayed with him for months. And each night, her screams had woken him. He would never forget the sound of his sister's screams.

"Ava, I'm sorry!" He immediately released her.

She staggered back.

Lights flooded on behind Grant. Scarlett was up; he knew she'd turned on those lights, and he could hear her footsteps racing toward him.

Ava was taking deep, gulping breaths. Her eyes were wide and terrified. All the color was gone from her cheeks, and her body trembled.

"I'm sorry," he said again, trying to make his voice sound soothing. He always tried to soothe Ava, but he never seemed to say or do the right thing with her. "I thought you were an intruder."

She flinched.

Hell. "Ava…"

She backed up a few more steps. Her gaze darted between him and Scarlett. "I didn't know anyone was here. I just…I needed a place to crash tonight."

He took a tentative step toward her. "You should be at college." She had only a semester to go before she graduated.

Ava swiped at her cheeks. "I needed to come home. I just…I needed to be here."

That wasn't like her. Usually, the last place she wanted to be was at the ranch.

"Hello, Ava," Scarlett said softly. "It's been a long time."

"Scarlett?"

Grant glanced over at Scarlett. She'd grabbed the sheet and wrapped it around her body.

Oh, hell, how awkward was this? He was wearing only jeans and Scarlett looked sexy as all hell wrapped in that sheet, with her hair tumbling around her shoulders.

"I'll, um, get dressed," she said as her cheeks flushed. She hurried back into the bedroom and shut the door behind her.

"Scarlett," Ava said, shaking her head. "Scarlett Stone? I remember her…I mean, she was ahead of me in school, but she was always around you."

No, I was always around her.

"I read about her in the paper." Ava had backed up a few more feet. "Did she kill her fiancé?"

Grant's back teeth locked. "No." He ran a hand over his jaw. "Scarlett is innocent, and we think we just caught the man who was framing her." He paused. Hell, he might as well tell her. "*After* he torched my place."

Her jaw dropped.

"That's why we're here," he said, giving a slow nod. "We needed a place to crash, too." He put his hands on his hips. "That's my excuse, Ava. What's yours?"

She looked away from him. "Sometime, it just gets to be…too much, you know? I feel like people are always whispering about me. Always watching me. I hate this place," she said starkly. "The ranch does nothing but make me hurt, but…at least no one here stares at me like I'm a freak."

"You're no freak." He marched to her side. Pulled her into his arms and held her tightly. She'd looked so shell-shocked, so broken when he'd flown from the Middle East, back to Austin. The docs had even put her in a psychiatric ward. And left her there.

I came back to take care of you. That was exactly what he would always do.

The door squeaked open behind him. He caught the scent of vanilla.

"I didn't do it," Ava whispered, the words so soft that he had to strain to hear her.

But they were words she'd said before. Words that pierced him to the heart right then, just as they had when he'd seen her in the psychiatric ward.

I didn't do it.

There was a reason he'd reacted so strongly when Scarlett had told him that she was being set up for murder. That she was innocent.

Most folks in the area thought his sister was guilty of murder, too. That she'd gotten away scot-free.

But he knew Ava was innocent. Just as he knew Scarlett was. And one day, he would find out who'd really killed his parents.

"I never thought you did," Grant said. But some people…some cops had been too quick with their suspicions. A girl at the scene right at the time of the kills? A girl who'd escaped without any injury at all? *She must be guilty. If she didn't do it herself, then she was in on the crime.*

The allegations had run rampant. And after all this time, those allegations still simmered with local law enforcement. *Until we find the real killers, there will always be some folks who think my sister murdered our parents.*

"I miss them so much." Ava's voice was still that soft whisper. "I keep thinking it will get better, but it never does."

He pressed a kiss to her temple.

She slid from his arms. Ava glanced over at Scarlett and winced. "I am so sorry. I never would have interrupted…come sneaking in like this if I thought—"

Scarlett lifted her hand. "This is your home, not mine. You don't need to apologize to me for anything."

Ava shook her head. "Still too nice, huh? That was always you."

Yes, it had been.

"I can go to the main house," Ava offered, but even as she said the words, terror flashed in her eyes.

"You know—" Scarlett was making her way to the small kitchen "—I think I could use some coffee. I mean, dawn isn't far off. Why not have a cup?"

Grant's brows rose.

Scarlett smiled at his sister. "It would be nice to catch up with you again. It really has been too long."

And Ava smiled back at her. "Yes, it has."

Grant watched them, realizing how at ease Ava seemed with Scarlett, and realizing *why*. When Scarlett looked at his sister, her eyes were warm. Her gaze was open. Friendly.

Not suspicious. Not judging. Scarlett knew exactly what it felt like to be suspected by those close to her, and she wasn't going to treat Ava that way.

She also wasn't going to turn Grant's sister away.

He rolled back his shoulders as he stared at them. Scarlett was poking at the coffeepot—the thing looked ancient—and saying it would be a miracle if they got anything drinkable from it.

Some of the shadows had lifted from Ava's eyes. She was still smiling at Scarlett.

His chest ached as he watched them. Two women who'd been falsely accused. Two women who'd been through hell.

But they'd come out stronger from their nightmares.

Two women…and he loved them both. In an instant, he would give his life for either of them.

IT WASN'T OVER.

Justin Turner was in the hospital, wailing for all to hear about his innocence. It was hard to buy an innocent act when the gas cans had been found in the fool's truck. A truck he'd *stolen* from a neighbor.

Sloppy work. Very sloppy.

It wasn't surprising that he'd been caught. Or shot. Grant McGuire wasn't the kind of man who'd just let his enemies slip away. He would want vengeance, payback from those who'd wronged him.

He could understand that. He wanted his payback, too.

What he couldn't understand was the man's attachment to Scarlett Stone. Grant should have been able to see her for exactly what she was.

The woman left a path of destruction in her wake. She never looked back to see the havoc she'd caused. She moved ahead, on to her next target.

She probably thought she was safe now, that the danger was over.

Her name would be cleared. Her job would be given back to her. The papers would paint her as the victim.

She'd get her life back. Scarlett would think that she'd gotten away from judgment.

She was dead wrong.

This wasn't the plan that had been in place for Scarlett. She should have suffered, should have lived her life behind bars, day in and day out. *That* would have been exactly what she deserved.

A fitting punishment.

But, no, things had changed now. Framing her wasn't an option. So if Scarlett's life couldn't be made into a living hell, well…

Then she just wouldn't get to live.

Chapter Ten

Scarlett walked outside, enjoying the view of the sun as it slowly rose into the sky. Her steps were slow and certain as she headed toward the bluff.

To Grant.

She saw him, standing with his legs braced apart, his hands by his sides, as he stared out at the water. His posture was so stiff and tense. Grant never seemed to relax. Or maybe it was just that the demons chasing him never let him rest.

She stopped a few feet behind him. "Your sister's changed a lot." Not the girl she remembered at all. A beautiful woman now, smart, warm, but with shadows in her eyes. *Just like her brothers.*

"You know the stories, don't you?" Grant was staring out at the water.

"Yes, but I never believed them."

He glanced back at her. "Is that why you came to me, telling me that you were innocent? You knew how I'd react, because of my sister?"

Scarlett shook her head and went to his side. She didn't touch him, just stood there, gazing at the view. "I went to you because…ten years ago, you stood out here with me. You broke my heart—"

He jerked. "Scarlett…"

"Well, you did." Why lie? "You broke my heart in one breath, and in the next you told me that if I ever needed you, you'd be there for me." She turned to face him. "I knew I could count on you, despite everything else. So that is why I went to you for help. We might not have made it as lovers, but we were always friends."

Pain flashed across his face.

"Tell me about them," she said, because she didn't want to talk about what she and Grant had lost. She wanted to try and take some of the shadows from his eyes. He'd helped her. He'd been there when she needed him most.

But what about when he needed someone? She wanted to help *him.*

His gaze slid toward the ranch house. She never looked away from him.

"I'd been gone for five months on my latest mission when I got the news. Five months, and I was on the other side of the world when they died." His words were low, and emotion simmered just beneath his surface. "They were at home—*you're supposed to be safe at home*—and they were killed. Intruders came in…and my parents were shot. Both at point-blank range." His breath rushed out. "It was two shooters. Their weapons were never found, and the bullets never matched up to any other crimes."

"Ava…"

"Ava was supposed to be at the homecoming dance that night, but she and her date had a fight at the last minute. She stayed here instead. *Here.* She was in the stables when she heard the first shot." His eyes shut.

Scarlett had read these details in the paper before, but hearing the pain in Grant's voice as he recounted the story made everything different.

"She ran to the house, spotted our mother on the floor…Ava could see her through the window. Our father—Ava says he saw her. That he shook his head when she tried to get closer. Then he started screaming, yelling at the shooters."

"What did he say?" Because that hadn't been in any newspaper account.

"He said, 'I'll never tell you. No matter what you do. *I'll never tell.*'"

Grant's eyes opened. "And Ava said they shot him. When she saw him fall, that's when she ran. She went back to the stables. Saddled her horse and didn't stop running until she got to the Montgomery ranch."

"She blames herself." That had been obvious to Scarlett.

He nodded. "She thinks she could have saved them. She doesn't get it…that if she'd gone in there, she would be dead, too."

Yes, Scarlett believed that Ava would have become just another target that night. "You think your father… you think he was trying to antagonize the shooter so he wouldn't see Ava? To keep the attackers focused just on him?"

Again, Grant nodded. "But his words are a clue, too. I think he knew the shooters. Ava didn't see their faces, but my dad did. He knew them. He knew exactly what they wanted." Grant's breath was a rough sigh. "They shot him, so we know they didn't get what they wanted from him." His voice lower, Grant added, "At least I hope the SOBs didn't get it. They ransacked the place, so we know they were searching hard for whatever it was they wanted that night."

Scarlett's gaze slid over the strong planes and angles of his face. "You came home then. You and your brothers."

"Ava was seventeen. We were her only family. Coming home, taking care of her—I owed her that. She was having nightmares, seeing attackers everywhere. She needed me." He lifted one shoulder. "I told my brothers that I would take care of things, but they came home, too. One at a time, they came, and we all found ourselves back in a city that we'd never been able to forget."

"You won't stop hunting for their killers."

"The police gave up. That's why we started digging on our own." Now a mocking smile lifted his lips. "We discovered that we were pretty good at hunting in the darkness."

"And you opened your PI firm."

"Take a group of ex-soldiers and put 'em together... we were bound to find some trouble."

The sun had risen higher into the sky. "The McGuire brothers were always good at finding trouble."

Grant laughed then, and the sound was so unexpected that Scarlett stilled. He had a deep, rumbling laugh, one that had always made her want to smile when she heard it.

But she hadn't heard his laugh in ten years.

"We all have our talents," he murmured.

Her heart ached then, because she thought of what could have been. Hopes she'd had so long ago.

She gave him a smile. Knew it would be both wistful and sad. "I think it's time for me to go." She wasn't just talking about leaving the ranch.

Scarlett turned away, but before she could take more than a few steps, he caught her hand.

"You got me through hell."

She didn't understand, and she shook her head.

His hand tightened around hers. "When the men next to me were dying, when I was sure the missions were unwinnable, when I couldn't even remember what it was like not to smell blood and death, *you* were the thing that kept me going."

"Grant—"

"What happens when you're afraid that you'll destroy the one thing you want most in the world?"

The question had her lips parting. "What are you talking about?" His touch seemed to burn her.

He glanced down at her hand, held so securely within his. "Are you going to pretend that you never saw it? When you saw *into* me, like no one else? The first time I looked into your eyes, I realized that you knew me... the real me."

She wanted to back away. Because she wanted to, she stepped closer to him.

"You knew that I liked the battles. The danger."

"The adrenaline," Scarlett whispered.

But he shook his head. "The first mission I was on...I realized I had a talent for what I was doing. Killing shouldn't be a talent, but it was for me. I excelled in the field. My senior officers noticed and word got passed along that I was the go-to for the most dangerous missions."

She wasn't sure what she was supposed to say.

His fingers slid up her wrist, trailing lightly over her racing pulse. "I was a hunter, Scarlett, straight to my soul. I fit in those battles. And with every mission, I know you saw what was happening to me."

She looked away from him.

"You did see it. You could always see everything about me."

Her lips pressed together. Then, because there should be no lies, she said, "Yes," and her voice was sad. But she had seen it. He'd stopped being the carefree boy. Become more intense. Darker.

Harder.

His edge had started to unnerve her.

"I could feel myself changing, and I didn't know how to stop. You—you were the bright spot for me. When I was with you, I wanted to be different. But I'd committed to another tour, one that was going to take me into the worst battle of my life. And I was afraid of who I'd be when I came back. I was afraid that I wasn't going to be the man you wanted anymore." His voice was ragged when he admitted, "I was afraid that I was becoming a monster."

"Grant, no." She grabbed his shoulders. "You were a hero. You saved lives!"

"I took lives, baby. And I think about them. Every. Single. One. I lost part of myself with those kills, and I don't think I'll ever be the same." His fingers slid from hers. "I didn't think you'd want who I was becoming."

She'd never realized Grant was the one who had so many doubts. Not strong, confident Grant.

"When I was at my weakest, when the blood was on the ground all around me, I thought of you. Only you. You were the one who got me out. Who gave me the strength to fight. To move. To damn well crawl if I had to do it." He leaned forward, and his forehead pressed to hers. "Because I wanted to see you again."

Then he'd come home…he'd come to look for her… and found Ian.

Life can be full of so many mistakes.

And…second chances?

Why should she be the one who was afraid this time? Why not take what she wanted so desperately? Take the chance that was right in front of her?

"You walked into my office days ago, and you were terrified. You know what I was?"

She had no clue.

"Glad to see you."

Now it was her turn to laugh.

"I had...followed you."

Her laughter faded away at his confession.

"The first restaurant was by chance. The second... I saw you go in, so I went there, too." Red stained his cheeks. "I wanted to see you, but you were engaged. You had a good life waiting, and I knew I should stay away from you. You, of all people, deserved to be happy."

But she hadn't been happy. Eric had been a good man, a good friend. But...

But the chemistry hadn't been there between them. She'd just never been able to feel the same for him.

The way I feel for Grant.

"I'm not the same man I was before. I don't want to be the same."

Her heart raced in her chest. "What do you want from me?"

"Everything." He said it so simply. So darkly. "And what do you want from me?"

Everything.

She glanced away from him.

Grant's phone rang then, the cry interrupting the tense silence that had fallen between them.

"Someone has bad timing," he growled. He yanked out his cell. Frowned at the screen. "Mac?"

"Mac" had to be Mackenzie McGuire. Mac had once been the wildest of the McGuire brothers, or at least, that had been the word from the women in town. Then he'd joined Delta Force and become both wild *and* deadly.

The furrow deepened between Grant's brows as he peered down at his phone. "He was doing some research for me on Ian Lake."

Ian?

He put the phone to his ears. "Mac? Look, they made an arrest last night—"

She didn't hear Mac's retort, but there was no missing the faint surprise that flickered over Grant's face. "I see." His voice was grim. "Thanks, man. I appreciate you being so thorough on this."

Scarlett rubbed her arms. She hadn't thought of Ian in years. He'd been a mistake. A guy who seemed too charming, but who'd been just hiding his true nature behind a facade. Grant had said that she could see into him, and maybe she had been able to do that.

But not with Ian. Ian had tricked her, at first.

"You flying back home?" Grant asked his brother.

Home. Her gaze slid around the ranch. Happiness and sorrow. They all wrapped together at that place.

"Good. I think…I think Ava could use some time with you."

Scarlett remembered that, years before, Ava had always followed Mac around. The two had been so close, often sharing secrets and laughter.

Ava doesn't laugh now.

The whole family was wounded, and Scarlett could see their pain—in their eyes, on their faces. When would they heal?

"Be safe," Grant told him. Then he shoved the phone back into his pocket. She saw the way he was studying her, as if he were trying to figure out how to break some bad news to her.

Scarlett sighed. She didn't want the man walking on eggshells around her. "Just spit it out, Grant."

The darkness lightened in his eyes. "Ian Lake wasn't behind the attacks on you."

"Well, um, that would be due to the fact that Justin Turner was the one the cops arrested last night."

"Ian Lake is dead."

Now she understood his surprise. "What happened?"

"He was killed in prison. Seems that he'd been arrested for assaulting his girlfriend. Before his family could help him to buy his way out of that mess—the way Mac said they'd apparently done in the past—he got into a fight with his cell mate. I guess this time he picked someone too big for him to shove around."

Her heartbeat quickened. "Mac is sure of this?"

"He checked the case files himself, questioned the officers who found Ian in that cell. He even went to the cemetery."

Thanks for being so thorough. Yes, that was Mac.

"He talked to a few other of Ian's ex's up there. Seems that you weren't the only girl who saw Ian's dark side." Grant lifted his hand, brushed her cheek.

"He hid it, at first, but I could see the cracks beneath his mask. After a while I finally saw him for what he was." And she'd left him. The cops hadn't believed her, not with Ian's buddy being more than willing to back up his story, but...

I took pictures of my injuries. I sent those pictures to Ian's parents. I wanted them to know exactly what their son was capable of doing. Scarlett had even included a note with those photos. Simple. Right to the point. *Stop him.*

It seemed they hadn't. They'd just covered up his crimes over the years.

"What do you see," Grant asked her, "when you look at me? Can you see beneath the cracks in my mask?"

She shook her head as his hand slid down to her shoul-der. "Is that what this is about? You think you're someone like Ian? Because you've been in battle and you've had to hurt other people?" She wanted to shake the man. "Yes, Grant, I see the danger in you. I always have. But you're a soldier. You're a protector. You're not a killer, and I have never been afraid of you."

Time to clear the air. No more fears from the past. No more longing for what couldn't be. "You want another chance with me? Not just sex, right?"

His lips quirked a bit. "Well, the sex is a fine bonus."

It was indeed. She cleared her throat. "Then let's do this. Me and you. We'll start over. Maybe we'll crash and burn, but maybe…maybe there can be a better ending for us this time."

She wasn't talking about forever. She was talking about one step at a time.

She offered him her hand. "Deal?"

His fingers closed around hers. "Deal."

THEY WERE LEAVING the ranch. Finally. That place was close to impenetrable, and after all the digging he'd done on McGuire's family, he knew why.

Trying to make sure you're safe? Not going to happen. No one could be safe all the time.

Just as no one could hide all the time. Grant and Scarlett were heading back to town. A meeting with the DA. The charges against Scarlett would be dismissed. It was just a matter of paperwork and time, and then she'd be a free woman.

Scarlett would think that she'd won. That she and Grant could be together.

No, Scarlett, that won't happen.

Grant McGuire was going to be a problem. He'd have to get him out of the picture in order to move in on Scarlett. Otherwise, the fool would just get in his way.

But that was okay, because eliminating Grant would serve to make Scarlett suffer all the more before her death.

Maybe she thought no one knew just how she felt about her military hero. He knew. He knew so much about her and Grant.

You are his weakness. And he is yours.

It was time to exploit those weaknesses.

He waited until they passed him in Grant's SUV. Then he pulled out behind them. The vehicle wasn't registered to him. Unlike Justin, he hadn't grabbed the first convenient ride he'd seen. He'd planned ahead. He always did.

The vehicle accelerated as he took off after his prey, and he smiled.

"WE SHOULD BE at the meeting with the DA by nine," Scarlett said. "That was the time Pierce gave me."

Grant shot a quick glance toward Scarlett. "After that…?"

"I'll be free."

He didn't want to crush her hope, but he knew the wheels of justice ground a lot slower than that. "The steps will start. Your name will be cleared soon."

He wondered how much information Shayne had been able to get out of Justin. Had the guy confessed during the long hours of the night?

"Do you think I'll be able to get my job back?"

"You will." He'd see to it.

His gaze slid back to the road. It stretched before him, lined with a few cars. Some of the vehicles vanished as they took the sharp curve up ahead.

A glance in his rearview mirror showed him a black SUV was coming up fast behind him. The guy needed to slow down. Everyone in that area knew how tricky the curve on 45 was. A few years back, some teenagers had been coming home from their prom, drunk on life and the booze they'd put into their punch bowl. They'd hit that curve too fast and tumbled into the ravine below.

Only one person had walked away from that accident.

But the SUV was still gaining on him. Still coming up too fast.

Grant's eyes narrowed as his instincts kicked into high gear. *This isn't right.*

"Grant?" Scarlett seemed to sense his concern. "Grant, what's happening?"

He wasn't going to speed ahead and rush into that curve. Not as treacherous as that spot was. *It's the perfect place to send someone careening over the edge.*

Instead of accelerating, he slowed.

Behind him, the SVU lurched forward

The other lane was empty, so Grant did a fast spin, turning their vehicle around and heading back toward the ranch.

If that was just some jerk hot-rodding on the road, he'd go straight past Grant now. If it wasn't some fool driving too fast, if it was someone intent on harm…

We're not at the curve.

They were heading down, about to pass right by that SUV.

"What's happening?" Scarlett demanded, her voice sharp. "I thought we were going to meet the DA."

They were.

That black SUV was still hurtling straight ahead. The windows were all darkly tinted, and Grant couldn't make out the driver at all.

The two vehicles were just about to pass one another when the SUV careened into Grant's side, slamming straight toward the driver's door.

The hit was hard, fast, brutal. Metal crunched, glass shattered and the air bags deployed in a sea of white.

Grant held tight to the wheel as he swerved to the right. His vehicle tipped off the side of the road.

The black SUV's engine roared as it raced away.

Grant shoved at the airbag. "Scarlett!" His left side throbbed and burned, and glass littered the area around him. No, the glass was on him, too.

"I'm okay." Her hand reached out for his. Held tight. "I'm okay, Grant! Are you?"

His left side felt wet, and the throbbing grew worse. He tried to pull away from the door, and felt the metal poking into him.

Grant turned his head and looked down the road. The black SUV had left a trail of broken glass in its wake, but the other vehicle was gone now, vanished around the curve.

The driver had sideswiped them, trying to give maximum injury to Grant's side of the vehicle. The SOB had succeeded.

"Call an ambulance," Grant told her.

Her hand tightened on his. "Grant?" Fear laced her voice.

He locked his jaw. He'd been shot before, twice, and he knew that he could get through this. He would get through this. The damn air bag was still in his way, so he couldn't see just how deep his injury was. He needed to see, to gauge how much damage had truly been done.

His shirt was already soaked with his blood.

He heard Scarlett talking then, but her voice seemed so far away. Then there was the rush of tires. Footsteps ran toward him.

"Buddy, buddy, are you okay?" a man's voice demanded. The guy tried to open Grant's door.

"Don't!" he barked, pain heavy in that one word.

"Grant." Now Scarlett's hand was on his shoulder. He tried to focus on her.

"Metal…from the door…in me." He could feel it. If they took that metal out, he might bleed even more. If it had hit something vital, and it sure seemed as if it might have, he could bleed out right in front of her. "Get… help…"

"Help's coming," she told him, her voice tight. "It's on the way." Her fingers still held his. She should get out of the vehicle. She'd be safer away from him then. What if the SUV came back? Grant couldn't protect her.

There were more voices, rising and falling. Women, men. Other drivers who were rushing over to try and assist. But they couldn't help him.

His left hand slid down. Part of the driver's door had twisted and the metal had shoved into him.

Had the SOB in that SUV been trying to kill me?

Strange…he hadn't been taken out in war zones. He'd made it out of battle again and again. But on this road, so close to home…

"I thought…thought he was going to try and push us at the curve." Grant wanted to explain to her why he'd turned around. *Trying to protect you.*

Her hand caressed his face. "It's okay. We're safe, Grant. We're safe." It sounded as if she was trying to reassure him. He'd wanted to reassure *her*. To protect her.

He'd failed.

"It impaled him," he heard one man mutter. "I can see it…right there."

Grant swallowed. His head turned. He saw Scarlett. Beautiful Scarlett. She was crying. She wasn't supposed to cry. She was supposed to be safe now. Happy.

"Second chance," Grant murmured. He wanted to kiss her. He'd always loved kissing Scarlett.

She nodded. A tear trickled down her cheek. "We have a second chance. This…it's just a scratch, Grant. Firefighters are coming. They'll bring—what do they bring?—the Jaws of Life," she rushed to say. "They'll get you out. You'll be fine."

Was she trying to convince him? Or herself?

He attempted to smile for her. He didn't want Scarlett to be scared. "Had…much worse before."

Another tear slid down her cheek.

He shook his head. "Don't…cry…for me. Shouldn't cry."

"Because you're going to be okay," she said, nodding. "You have to be okay, Grant."

He did. He would be. It was just…he felt so cold.

It was hot in Texas. There was no reason for the cold.

Metal groaned near him. Was someone still trying to open the door? *"Don't let them move it. Scarlett… don't…"*

"Grant? Grant, look at me."

He hadn't realized that his eyes had closed.

"You're the strongest man I know. You hold on, do you hear me? You keep those eyes open and on me. You see me. *See me.*"

He smiled at her. At least he thought he did. "You always saw me. Scared me, the way you saw…so deep."

"Grant?"

"Did you see…that I loved you?"

Her breath choked out. "You are *not* making some death-scene confession. I will not have that, do you understand?"

His Scarlett. Always making him smile.

But he couldn't see her anymore.

"Grant?"

"I hope…you saw…"

He couldn't see anything at all.

Chapter Eleven

The doctors and nurses rushed the gurney through the emergency room doors. Scarlett had been racing with them, had been at Grant's side every moment since the attack, but a nurse turned back and caught her shoulders.

"Ma'am, I'm sorry, but you can't go in there."

"He needs me!" *I need him.*

"He needs medical care." Sympathy laced the woman's voice. "The doctors are going to take care of him. Just stay here, and I'll update you as soon as I can."

She pulled away.

"Please—" Scarlett's voice broke.

The nurse looked at her.

"Take care of him? Make him…make him all right again."

The woman's face softened. "We'll do everything that we can."

And then she was gone.

Scarlett stood in the middle of the ER waiting room, her shoulders hunched as she tried to keep the tears from falling. She'd never seen Grant like that. So still. So pale. When the firefighters had finally cut him out of the vehicle, when she'd seen just how deeply that metal had twisted into him…

Grant, how were you even talking to me?

She looked down at her hands. There was blood there. His blood. His SUV had been nearly destroyed on the driver's side, but she'd come away without so much as a scratch.

This wasn't supposed to happen. They were supposed to be past the danger. Some maniac in a too-fast vehicle wasn't supposed to take Grant's life away.

"Miss?" A nurse behind the check-in counter was frowning at her. "Is there…is there someone I can call for you?"

Grant's family. She needed to call them. To tell them what had happened.

But she couldn't seem to move. She could only stare at the blood on her hands and think—

I can't lose him.

Not when he'd just come back into her life again. It wasn't about a second chance. It was about their only chance. And she couldn't lose him.

"Miss?"

Stay strong. Grant needs you. Stay. Strong.

She put her hands down. The blood had smeared over her clothes. His blood. Scarlett swallowed. "His family. The McGuires. I have to call them." They needed to all be there when Grant came out of surgery.

Because he would pull through. There was no alternative for her.

Putting one foot in front of the other, Scarlett made herself move toward the counter. She needed to contact his family, but…

What is their number? Her fingers trembled. She'd lost touch with them all over the years, and didn't even know their number. She didn't know—

"Scarlett?"

She turned at the familiar voice and saw Detective

Townsend standing just a few feet away. He frowned at her. "What's wrong? What are you doing here?" His gaze raked her and shock filled his eyes.

"It's Grant." *Don't break. Stay focused.* "He's hurt. I need to reach his family, but I..." Shame filled her. *I don't even know their numbers.*

Shayne pulled out his phone. Dialed fast. "Brodie? Yeah, it's Shayne. Get the family to St. Benedict's Hospital right away." There was a stark pause. "Grant's hurt."

And apparently, that was all he needed to say, because he lowered the phone back down.

"They're coming," he said simply.

She lifted her chin. "Thank you."

He closed the distance between them, moving slowly, as if afraid he'd spook her. "That's a lot of blood, Scarlett. Do you need help, too?"

She shook her head. "It's all his."

The detective took her hand. Pulled her away from the check-in desk. "What happened?"

Shayne...he'd been doing his job all along, she knew. Unfortunately, his job had involved trying to pin a murder on her.

"I've known Grant a long time," he told her softly. "We're friends, though you may not believe that."

Her eyelashes flickered.

"Talk to me."

Her breath slid out. "We were going into town. To meet with the DA—"

The furrow between his brows deepened. "You had a meeting with the DA?"

"Yes, my lawyer called us. He said..." She stopped. That didn't matter right then. "A black SUV was following us. He hit Grant's side of the vehicle and..." Her voice dropped. "It's bad." Those two words were stark. Scared.

"The metal went through his side. We couldn't get him out of the vehicle, and the blood…" Her gaze fell to her hands once more. "I need to get it off. Please."

His hands tightened around her. "It's all right. We'll take care of you." He pulled her with him.

Her gaze slid to the ER doors. Grant was back there. "He's going to be okay," she heard herself say.

"Hell, yes, he will be. Grant McGuire isn't about to let death take him." Shayne sounded absolutely certain. "He's not about to let anyone or anything take him away from *you*."

Her gaze flew to him.

But Shayne just shook his head. "I've seen the way he looks at you, and I've been with Grant a few times when he got drunk and desperate. You've been in that man's head for years. Now that you're back in his life, there's no way he's giving you up."

Her eyes widened in surprise. Shayne had known about her and Grant all along? And he hadn't said anything.

"My instincts are usually pretty good about people," he told her. "And I didn't think you were a killer, despite what the evidence was trying to tell me."

Her breath whispered out.

"He's going to be all right," Shayne told her.

This time, it almost sounded as if he was trying to convince himself.

THE WAITING ROOM was full of McGuires. They weren't in the ER any longer. Grant was in surgery, and they were camped out, waiting to hear from his doctor.

Brodie was pacing, moving restlessly like a caged lion. Davis was stone still as he stared out the window. Sullivan kept grilling the nurses in three-minute intervals.

Ava sat next to Shayne. The detective shot her worried frowns every few moments, and he even awkwardly patted her hand a few times.

Mac was on the way. He'd caught a flight out of Atlanta, and had told them that he'd be there as soon as he could.

The surgery was taking too long. Scarlett knew that. But then, she'd known this would be more intense than a simple stitch-up.

She sat with her eyes directed straight on the OR doors. When those doors opened and the doctor came out, she wanted to see him first thing.

"Where's Justin Turner?" The low, growling voice belonged to Sullivan. He'd turned away from the nurses and had closed in on Shayne.

Scarlett didn't look at them. She kept staring at the doors, willing them to open.

"He's upstairs. Third floor. I've got two guards on him." Shayne sounded weary, and Scarlett realized he must have been at the hospital, grilling Justin, nearly all night. "I was just leaving when I saw Scarlett."

The hospital's main parking lot was just beyond the emergency room entrance.

"If he's the killer," Sullivan demanded, "then how come my brother was targeted today?"

And it had been an attack targeted right at Grant. His side of the vehicle.

The image flashed before her mind, of Grant pinned in that SUV, but she shoved it away. Kept staring at those doors.

"Your brother investigates a lot of cases. You all do." Shayne's answer was low, and Scarlett had to strain in order to hear him. "Maybe this isn't about Scarlett at all. Maybe it's about something else. Someone else." He paused. "You can bet I'll find out what's happening," he finished grimly.

"We'll find out," Sullivan swore. Then he paced toward Scarlett. She tensed, expecting him to start interrogating her once more. He'd done that before. Asking her, again and again, about the driver. Had she seen him? Had she seen the tag on the vehicle? When had they first noticed the SUV? Was the driver swerving the whole time or had he come at them deliberately?

She'd had no doubt that it had been a deliberate attack.

"How are you holding up?" Sullivan's voice was... soft, for Sullivan. Concerned.

And her eyes slid away from those OR doors. She stared up at him. His eyes didn't look so hard then. Real emotion shone back at her.

For an instant, he wasn't *Sullivan*...he was the boy she remembered from school. Her friend. Sully.

He didn't wait for her to answer. Instead, he slid into the seat next to her. It creaked beneath him. He took her hand. Squeezed. "You know I hate hospitals." His voice carried only to her. "Because every time I come into a place like this, I remember you."

Her brows lifted.

"I wanted to help you that day, but there was nothing I could do. You were hurting—hell, it was far past hurt." His fingers tightened on hers. "And then...you just walked away. By yourself. You walked out of the hospital and I just watched you."

"Sully..." His old nickname slipped from her. The nickname that only friends and family ever used.

"We've been friends, of a sort, for most of our lives."

She swallowed. Yes, despite everything, she did think of Sullivan that way. He'd seen her at her worst, again and again.

"My brother has loved you since the first moment he saw you. I know…because I saw just how lost and confused he got when he was with you. He thought his life was going to be one thing…and then…there was you."

Scarlett wasn't sure she wanted to hear more.

"He never thought he deserved you." Those words were almost whispered. "Not with the blood on his hands."

His blood had stained her hands today.

"But he wanted you, more than he ever wanted anything."

Her gaze slid back to those doors.

"I know that you've always had the power to wreck my brother. You probably don't realize it, but you do. Because even when he wasn't with you, he was holding on to the *idea* of you. Hell, if you look in his wallet, you'll even find that old prom picture of you two. I'm pretty sure he took that to every hellhole he survived."

You were with me. Grant's words drifted through her mind.

He'd been with her, too. Always in her heart.

"I just…I thought you should know." Sullivan's voice was gruff. He started to rise.

She caught his hand. Curled her fingers around his wrist. "You're not my friend, Sully."

He flinched. Pain flashed for a moment in his eyes, but then was quickly hidden. "Right. I overstepped. Sorry, I didn't mean to assume—"

"You're more," she said simply. "You scare me, you infuriate me, but…you've always been there for me." Her lips lifted. "You're like the very, very scary brother who comes out when I need him most."

His eyes widened.

"My life wouldn't be the same without you. And that

night, in this hospital when I lost the baby…" This same damn hospital. "I was glad that you were here." Because she hadn't wanted to be alone then.

He nodded. His eyes had lightened.

She became aware of the silence then. Sully's voice had been pitched low, for her ears alone, but Scarlett hadn't hushed her own words. She glanced around and saw that all the McGuires—and Shayne—were watching them.

"Well…" Brodie stopped his pacing. "What do I have to do in order to become your brother?"

"That's easy," Davis said, before she could think of a reply. "Get Grant to marry her, then we're all in."

Marry Grant?

The OR doors opened then. She leaped to her feet and raced Sully to the doctor. She beat him by seconds as she staggered to a stop. "Grant!" His name burst from her. "Is he—"

The doctor frowned at her. "Are you family, ma'am?"

He hadn't been one of the doctors she'd seen before. He didn't know—

"She's family," Sully said flatly. "We all are. Now… *how is he?*"

Rolling his shoulders, the doctor said, "There was extensive internal damage, but we were able to stop the bleeding. The man in there is exceptionally lucky. If that metal had gone in even another inch, there would have been nothing we could do."

Don't let them move the door. Scarlett…don't…

She swiped at the tears on her cheeks.

"He's going to need a few days to recover, and the man will have to take it easy for a while after that." A smile lit the doctor's face. "But he's going to be just fine."

Yes! Scarlett grabbed Sully and hugged him tightly. He held her just as fiercely.

Then she shoved him away and whirled toward the doctor once more. "When can I see him?"

"He's in recovery. He's not awake, and probably won't be for quite some time, but you can go in for a bit. Sometimes having family close by helps the recovery process." His gaze swept the assembled crowd. "But only two at a time. No more, understand?"

She understood Grant was going to be all right. The fear that had grabbed so tightly to her finally began to ease.

HE WAS CONNECTED to tubes. Machines. A steady beeping filled the recovery area as Scarlett crept toward the bed. Ava was with her, moving just as slowly and gingerly.

Grant's lashes were closed. Stark white hospital sheets were pulled to his hips. He looked pale, and dark shadows lay beneath his closed lashes.

He's alive.

"Grant always seems so strong." Ava's voice was halting as she approached the bed. "Sometimes I forget that he's just like the rest of us. He can get hurt. He can—"

"He is strong," Scarlett said, cutting through her words. She knew exactly what Ava had been about to say. *He can die.* No, he *wasn't* dying. Not today. Not anytime soon. She ran her fingers lightly over the back of his hand. An IV was attached there, and she tried to be careful, not wanting to pull on the tape.

His eyelashes seemed to flicker.

"Second chances, Grant," she whispered as she leaned toward him. Her lips brushed lightly over his cheek. "It looks like you just got another one."

SULLIVAN TURNED AWAY from the recovery room. His brother was going to make it. Sullivan had never doubted it.

Even if fear had snaked around his heart.

"Aren't you going in?" Brodie asked him, frowning.

"It's not me he'll want to see." The person who'd make his brother wake up and recover? Yeah, that would be Scarlett. For Scarlett, Grant would do just about anything.

Even sentence himself to years of pain because the fool thought she deserved someone "better."

His gaze slid to the right. Shayne Townsend was there. Leaning against the back wall as the cop called someone on his phone.

Sullivan stalked toward him.

"Yeah, yeah," Shayne was saying. "She thought she was meeting with the DA this morning. I don't know why. Someone got their wires crossed." He paused a beat. His stare sharpened on Sullivan. "I want a full report on that accident scene. I know it's not my case, I don't care— send me what you find out." He ended the call. Frowned at Sullivan. "Is everything—"

"Justin Turner is on the third floor, that's what you said?"

He nodded.

"And he has guards?" The guards would be a problem.

Again, Shayne nodded.

"I need you to get me past those guards," Sullivan said, his voice soft but implacable. "I want to talk to him."

"That can't happen, man. He's under arrest—"

"For torching my brother's house. Right. Got it. But seeing as how my brother was just nearly killed, you can see where I might want to have a little…one-on-one meeting with Justin." Sullivan crossed his arms over his chest. "Maybe the guy wasn't working alone." He knew the same thought had no doubt occurred to the cop. "If someone else is planning to attack again, if he's hired someone to come after Grant and Scarlett, I will find out." Because he didn't have to play by the rules like the good old cop did. "Give me five minutes, and I'll have everything I need to know."

Shayne hesitated.

"Five minutes," Sullivan said. It wasn't a plea.

It was an order.

Because he knew some of the secrets that Shayne Townsend carried, and he wasn't above using those secrets as leverage in order to get what he wanted.

The detective's eyes narrowed with a burst of fury. He obviously knew just what Sullivan was saying—and what he wasn't. After a moment, Shayne gave a tense nod. "Five minutes, but you can't leave a mark on him."

Sullivan laughed at that. "I never do." It wasn't amateur hour.

Silently, he followed the cop to the elevator. He turned back just before the doors closed, and saw Scarlett. She'd left the recovery room. Brodie and Davis were heading in for their turns with Grant then.

My brother shouldn't be in that little room. Scarlett shouldn't still have Grant's blood on her shirt.

She stepped toward him. "Sully?"

The elevator doors slid closed.

There were times when someone needed to do the dirty work. Sullivan had become good at that particular task. He was an expert at it, of sorts. Thanks in large part to Uncle Sam's training.

He'd get the answers he needed, one way or another.

HE HURT.

The pain was the first awareness that Grant had. It pulsed through his side, throbbing, aching. But pain was a good thing. The soldier in him knew that. If he felt pain, that meant he was still alive. And if he was alive...

"Scarlett." Her name emerged as a whisper. He tried to push open his eyelids. They didn't exactly want to cooperate, and that just made him all the more determined to see—

"I'm here."

Her.

His eyes opened. At first, everything was unfocused. Soft white, foggy. But he blinked a few times and the hospital room crystalized for him. And Scarlett was there, sitting near his bed. Her fingers twined with his.

She smiled when their eyes met, and it was a smile that lit up her whole face.

It was the smile she used to give to him, a lifetime before.

Nearly dying had totally been worth the price to see that smile. "Told you..." he managed to say "...I'd be all right."

Her laughter held a desperate edge. "All right? Don't even ask me how long it took them to stitch you up." Her fingers tightened around his. "You were far from all right, Grant."

He tried to shrug. Didn't happen. But the machines around him starting doing a double-time beat. "Just a scratch."

"Tell that to someone who didn't see all the blood you lost." And her smile was gone. Shadows lined her eyes. "I was scared."

He wanted to pull her into his arms and hold her. But he was hooked up to so many wires and needles. "I wasn't going to leave you."

She stood then, and he thought for an instant that she was about to leave him. But she leaned over him instead.

Her lips brushed his. "How about," she whispered against his mouth, "you don't ever do that again?"

It wasn't exactly on his to-do list. "Yes, ma'am," he managed to reply, and the words sounded only a little bit hoarse.

Her lips pressed to his once more. Then she pulled back to stare at him. "Just how much do you remember?"

His eyes narrowed. "I remember…the black SUV." His instincts had been screaming at him as soon as he saw the accelerating vehicle in his rearview mirror. "It…hit us."

"It swerved and slammed into the driver's side." Her voice shook. "The metal twisted, the windows shattered, and you were—"

"Trapped." Yes, he did remember that. The pain in his side had reminded him. He looked down, because he had to see the damage, but when he pulled aside the sheet, all he saw was a big, thick, white bandage.

"You'll have a new scar to add to your collection."

So he would. He lowered the sheet.

"Do you remember anything else?"

There was a hesitant note in her voice. He strained, struggling to remember. "The air bag deployed. It was like a white cloud all around me."

She nodded. And waited.

What else had happened? "What?" he asked, hating the rough sound of his voice. "Did I do…something? What is it?"

Scarlett opened her mouth to reply, then hesitated.

"Scarlett?"

She smiled. A sweet, almost sad smile. "You almost died on me," she told him. "And I realized that I didn't want to be without you."

Was she saying…?

"Second chances," Scarlett whispered.

And he had a flash of her face. Tears had been on her cheeks. Blood had been on the hands that touched him. She'd been talking to him. Telling him that he'd be all right.

The door opened with a faint squeak. Footsteps padded into the room. Grant didn't look away from Scarlett.

There was something that she was holding back from him.

"Well, well. I get word that my brother is supposed to be at death's door," a mocking voice said. "And I rush here to find him wide-awake, with a pretty woman already in his bed."

Scarlett's cheeks stained because—Grant glanced down—yes, she was in bed with him.

Pretty much, anyway.

"Mac…" He growled out his brother's name as Scarlett turned toward the man who'd just entered the room.

Mac had their father's dark hair and the McGuire family green eyes. A faint scar sliced through his right eyebrow, and another notched under the cleft in his chin. He was smiling as he approached, and that smile lit his eyes.

"Brodie had me fearing the worst," he muttered as he neared the bed. Mac shook his head. "And I couldn't get here fast enough."

Grant had felt the same way before. When he'd gotten the news about his parents, he hadn't been able to return fast enough. He'd been a world away, and his life had crumbled.

"Glad you're okay," Mac said. He leaned down and clapped a hand on Grant's shoulder. "Now don't ever pull that crap again, got it?"

As if Mac was one to talk. His scar collection was unrivaled. He liked the dangerous missions. The more difficult the odds, the more he reveled in the cases.

Mac glanced over at Scarlett. "Heard you were with him when it happened."

"Yes," she whispered.

"Tell me that you saw the SOB." Lethal intent was in his voice.

Scarlett shook her head. "I'm sorry." Her gaze slid back to Grant. "His windows were tinted too dark. I couldn't see into his SUV. It just—it all happened so fast. He slammed into Grant's side and was gone in an instant—"

"So he meant to hit Grant?"

"Yes." Her voice was certain. Grant was just as certain. That had been no drunk driver. No chance car accident.

The driver of that SUV had wanted to kill him.

He'd nearly succeeded.

The faint lines near Mac's eyes tightened. "A new day, a new enemy? Is that how it's going for you, Grant?"

It sure felt that way.

"We'll figure this out." Scarlett's hand brushed over Grant's forehead. "You just need to rest now. You were only moved to this private room a few hours ago. The doctor said that you'd need to recover for a few days."

He didn't want to lie in bed and recover. He wanted to be out, hunting down the guy who'd gone after him. With every moment that passed, the trail left by the fellow would be growing colder and colder. "Mac…"

"Oh, you can count on me," his brother said with a nod, obviously understanding. "I'll go talk to the cops who investigated the scene and find out just what they know."

Good. And he'd—

Scarlett's fingers pushed against his chest. "You are not seriously trying to get out of that bed!"

Um, he might have been trying just that.

She pressed the call button for the nurse. "You aren't indestructible, no matter what you might think. You lost too much blood. You nearly *died*."

The door opened again. This time, Sullivan's familiar face appeared. He was frowning, until he saw Grant, and when he saw Scarlett *pushing* Grant back down onto the bed, one of his rare smiles lit his face.

"Back with the living?" he asked. "I mean, really back…because a time or two there, you woke up talking all crazy. I think you even asked Scarlett to marry you."

Her hands flew away from him. "You didn't."

But there was *something* there…in her eyes. Grant caught her hand. "I don't think that sounds so crazy."

She licked her lips. "You need to rest. I need you to rest."

"Listen to the lady," Mac advised curtly. "I'll start the hunt. You know you can count on me."

He did. He could count on all his family members—always.

"I'll start with that Justin Turner." Mac gave a grim nod. "He torches your place one night, and the next, some bozo tries to run you over? Hell of a coincidence. I'm thinking he's got a partner, or he hired someone to—"

"I already had a little chat with dear Justin."

Sullivan's words captured Grant's total attention.

Sully's eyes held his. "And we've got a problem. A very, very big problem." He shook his head. "He's not our guy."

"What?" Scarlett took a step toward him. "Of course he's our guy! We caught the man red-handed. The gas tanks were in the stolen pickup truck that he'd driven to Grant's."

"Oh, he set the blaze at Grant's home. The guy admitted that to me." Sully paused. "But he didn't kill his brother. He swears it. And he swears he wasn't behind the frame-up on you, Scarlett."

Grant saw her fingers clench into fists.

"And you believe him?" she asked.

"Let's just say that the guy realized it was in his best interest to tell me the truth. The complete truth."

And Grant understood that Sullivan had been using his "special" interrogation techniques. "Damn it, Sully—" The last thing they needed was for him to wind up under arrest.

"I didn't leave a mark on him," Sullivan murmured, "and I got him to confess all to me. He had huge gambling debts, and the guy's an alcoholic."

After their last few encounters, Grant had suspected that.

"When Eric threatened to cut him off financially, Justin panicked. He thought for sure Scarlett was the reason his brother was getting so tight with the purse strings."

"I wasn't," she declared. "I didn't even know about that money!"

The stitches pulled in Grant's side as he shifted on the bed.

"When Eric died, the guy's financial troubles were over, but Justin's guilt set in, hard. He thought Scarlett was going to get away with killing his brother, and he wanted to do anything necessary to bring her to justice."

"You're kidding me." She shook her head. "He burned Grant's house to the ground. He—"

"Said he did it to draw you out. To show Grant that you were dangerous. He thinks that you destroy every man you touch."

Scarlett flinched. "Well, why not just write that on a greeting card?" She edged away from Grant.

He wanted her back at his side.

"From what I can tell, he hasn't been sober in years—"

"So how do you know he isn't lying?" Scarlett managed to ask. "How do you know—"

"His hand," Sully said flatly.

Grant frowned. The pain was growing worse, and the nurse had just bustled into his room, a young redhead with a broad smile. "You're awake!" she exclaimed, sounding cheerful…and so at odds with everyone else there, who basically ignored her.

"Justin's fingers shake. Probably from all the alcohol the guy's had in his system. Maybe from something else." Sullivan exhaled. "They tremble constantly. You must have seen it."

Grant frowned, and he remembered the guy's shaking fingers. He *had* seen the tremble.

"So? What does that matter?" Scarlett asked, her voice rising. "He's dangerous—"

The nurse's smile dimmed a bit as she glanced around the room.

"He is," Sullivan agreed.

"Damn straight," Mac added.

"But he isn't the man who killed Eric with a knife. He isn't the man who murdered Louis East in that alley."

The nurse edged back a step.

"And I'm guessing the man who came at you in the dark…Scarlett, were his fingers shaking as he held that knife to you?"

She shook her head.

"Justin Turner can't even hold a knife. He can't hold it steady." Sullivan's gaze swept toward Grant. "Justin may be a fire-burning SOB, but he's not the killer we're after. The man who killed those others…the man who came after Scarlett…he's still out there." He gave a hard nod. "And I think he's the same man who tried to take you out on that road."

Hell. The danger was far from over. "I want out of this bed," Grant growled.

No one moved.

"Now!" Because he wasn't going to stay here while that killer was out there, hunting Scarlett, hunting him. The guy would attack again. Grant couldn't be weak while that predator was on the loose.

The nurse bustled toward him. His machines were beeping loudly.

"Way to rile him up," Mac muttered to Sullivan. "Great job, jerk."

Sullivan swore.

The nurse put her hands on Grant's arms. "Sir, you have to calm down or you will tear out those stitches." She lifted a syringe. Aimed for his IV. "It's time for your next dosage of pain medication."

"No!" Grant shook his head. "That will make me sleep. I can't sleep. I have to…I have to be ready."

But Scarlett was beside him once more. "No, you don't. The battle's over, soldier." Her voice was soft, her face tender as she stared down at him.

The war was still raging. She had to see that. The danger was closing in, and he had to protect her.

It's not over.

An image of that black SUV flashed before his eyes.

Chapter Twelve

Scarlett slipped from Grant's room, aware that her knees were shaking. *He's all right. He's all right.* The mantra repeated through her mind as she eased down the hallway and took deep gulps of air. She'd been so worried about Grant, and the cold vise around her heart hadn't eased, not until he'd whispered her name and opened his eyes.

She'd tried to fool herself into thinking that, during the past few days, she'd kept her emotions closed off. That she wasn't still vulnerable to him. She'd realized that lie for what it was the instant their vehicle had spun off the road.

Grant mattered to her. He'd always mattered. Time and space hadn't changed the way she felt for him. Nothing could change it.

Did you see...that I loved you?

His question had pierced Scarlett to her core.

I hope...you saw it.

"Scarlett?"

She turned at the call, her hands knotting into fists.

"Scarlett, is everything okay?" Shayne asked as he shuffled closer to her. "Grant hasn't taken a turn for the worse, has he?"

She straightened her shoulders. Pasted a smile on her face. "He's actually awake." And trying to fight off the nurse. "He's going to be fine. He's—he's in there with his brothers now."

Shayne's gaze swept over her face. "Then why are you out here, looking as if you just lost your best friend?"

Because I'm afraid. I thought the nightmare was over, and it isn't.

"Sullivan," Shayne growled in the next instant. "He's one of the brothers in there, right? And he told you about Justin."

She swallowed to ease the dryness in her throat. "Is Sullivan right? Or do you think Justin was behind those murders?"

"I'm…looking into other possibilities," the detective said, the words slow and careful and not what she wanted to hear.

"But if it's not Justin, then it could be anyone." The nightmare would just keep going. "I want this to be over! I want to be safe."

"Safety's an illusion."

Confused, Scarlett shook her head.

"We walk around, thinking that the threats aren't out there, but they always are." Shayne's eyes were grim. "If you'd seen the cases that have crossed my desk, you'd know that no one is really safe."

That was hardly reassuring.

She rubbed her chilled arms. Hospitals always felt so cold, and this one in particular left her chilled to the bone.

"But we will find this guy. We've got an APB out for that black SUV. One of the witnesses on scene was able to give us the first three digits of the license plate, and it's only a matter of time until we find the perp."

"Time…" Anger pushed through her fear. "What if during that *time*, he attacks again? Only Grant might not survive another attack. Or maybe I won't. I can't just stand around and wait for this guy to come at me!"

The door opened behind her. Sullivan stood there. Sullivan who feared nothing and no one.

"I think you should be placed in protective custody," Shayne said.

What?

"And I'm putting a guard on Grant. He'll be monitored 24-7, so you can be assured of his safety."

Sullivan strode toward them. "We already are assured of that. Mac has the first watch on him, and Brodie will be taking the second shift." Sully flashed Shayne a tiger's smile, cold and deadly. "We guard our own, and you can be assured of that."

The McGuires would look after one another, Scarlett knew. Her breath came a bit easier.

"My man will be there, too," Shayne said, his words with an edge. Then his voice softened as he turned back to Scarlett. "I can take you to a safe house. You can stay there, guarded and secure, until we catch this guy."

But what if they didn't catch him? Not for a week, a month, a year?

What if they never caught him?

Shaking her head, she backed away from Shayne. "Grant needs me."

"He was already calling for you when I left," Sullivan murmured.

Her chin lifted. "And I need him. I won't leave him on his own." Okay, not on his own—not with all those brothers around. *Hardly alone.* "I won't leave him," she said again, "not when he's hurt."

I won't leave him at all. She'd just gotten him back. Just realized that the love she'd had for him still stirred as strongly in her heart. She wasn't about to lose this new chance. *Their new chance.*

She nodded to the cop then turned back toward Grant's room. No matter what, she wouldn't let Grant see the fear growing within her.

Together, we'll face this. Whatever the SOB is planning...we'll face him together.

Scarlett was dead.

Grant held her body in his arms. Her blood was on him, her eyes were closed, and no matter how many times he called her name, she was just...gone.

And he could hear the growl of an engine. He looked up and was pinned in the bright lights of a big, dark SUV. An SUV that was rushing right toward him as he stood, cradling Scarlett, in the middle of that long, lonely road.

The oncoming lights grew brighter. The SUV rushed ever closer. He whirled, trying to brace for the impact that would come, even as he held her tighter in his arms.

I'm sorry, Scarlett.

"Grant!" Scarlett's worried voice called to him.

He blinked, and the nightmare vanished.

Not dead. Not dead. Not. Scarlett's hand was on his shoulder. She stared at him with wide eyes. "You were crying out. It's okay. You're safe here, Grant. I think...I think you were having a bad dream."

Not just a dream, but a reality that *could* be.

I won't lose her.

He caught her hand. Brought it to his lips. Kissed her fingers.

Sweat had slickened his body. The meds—they were messing with his mind.

"Do you want to talk about it?" Her voice was so soft.

He shook his head. The last thing he wanted was to relive that hell.

The beeping machines slowed as his racing heartbeat quieted.

"Are you in pain?"

Only when she wasn't with him. "No."

But she pulled away from him. Sat near the bed. Watched him with her dark eyes.

She was seeing into him again.

He wanted her to learn all his secrets this time. Because he was tired of carrying them around.

"Do you still love me, Grant?"

The ache he felt then had nothing to do with his injury. He turned his head to see her better. Then, staring into her eyes, he told her the simple truth. "I never stopped."

He heard the rasp of her breath.

"Scarlett, I—"

A phone rang then. Its peal loud and close.

"That's my phone," she murmured, glancing to the side. "One of your brothers brought it by for me. Davis. He thought I might need it. I'd left it at the crash scene."

But she didn't answer the call. She just kept staring at him.

And the phone kept ringing.

"Answer it," he told her softly. *I'm not going anywhere. Not now.*

Not ever.

She reached for the phone. "My lawyer." Horror flashed across her face. "The DA!" Then she was fumbling and answering the phone. "Pierce, I'm sorry I missed the meeting yesterday! Grant's in the hospital, and I've been with him the whole time—"

She broke off, tilting her head as she listened to his response.

"I don't think I can come," she said, exhaling slowly. "No, no, I need to be with Grant."

He frowned as he listened to her.

"Bring the paperwork here," she told him. "Can you do that? Good. Thank you. And just…call me when you arrive, okay? I'll come and meet you in the lobby."

Then she put the phone back down.

"There was a mix-up," she said, her head lowered and the curtain of her hair shielded her eyes. "The DA had to leave the office anyway, and she meant to reschedule but…but *I'm free*." Her head lifted. Red stained her cheeks. "Pierce says it's just a matter of me signing some paperwork, and all the charges will be dismissed against me. He's coming over here. He says the DA is with him and we can go over the material together. After I sign some forms, then they'll present everything to the judge next week."

She rose from her chair, then leaned forward and hugged him. "I'm free!"

Her scent surrounded him.

"Thank you," she whispered. "You believed in me, always." She pulled back, just a little, and their mouths were kissing-close. She gazed into his eyes. "Why did you always believe in me?"

Wasn't that obvious? "I told you…I love you."

She shook her head.

"I. Love. You." He thought for sure that she'd seen it. He'd been crazy from the moment she'd walked back into his life. Stumbling over his words, nearly baring his battered soul again and again for her.

"Austin. Afghanistan. Russia. Egypt. It didn't matter where I was, you were in my mind. Always in my heart. You. Even when I knew that you should be with someone else, someone…hell, someone with a soul that didn't always feel bloodstained, I never stopped loving you." The simple truth was… "I couldn't stop." Loving her was as natural and basic for him as breathing.

She licked her lips. "I couldn't stop, either."

No, no, she hadn't just said—

"Grant McGuire, I fell in love with you when I was a teenager, and I never stopped. Austin. Atlanta. Wherever I went—" she pulled in a deep breath "—you were in my heart, too. And always in my dreams. I wondered where you were, and I prayed that you were safe."

He shook his head. There was no way he'd heard her right. That pain medicine was definitely messing with him.

"When my life was on the line, you were the first person that I thought of. I knew you would be there for me. I knew I could count on you. There are some things that time can't change."

He wanted to kiss her. Wanted to sink into her, to wrap around her and never let go.

"Second chances," she said.

He nodded.

"I want mine. I want ours."

"We have it," he swore.

Then she leaned toward him. Her lips brushed over his. The kiss was the sweetest he'd ever had. It tasted of her and of hope.

Of love.

I don't know why you love me, Scarlett, but I swear, I'll prove that I'm a man worthy of you. Even if it took him the rest of his life, he'd prove himself to her.

The kiss was slow, tender, but the machines started to beep again. Faster. Louder.

The door swung open.

"I'm getting an alert—" the nurse began.

Grant and Scarlett turned toward her. It was the same redhead from before. Her mouth snapped closed. "That's why the machines are going off." She pointed her finger at them. "That needs to wait."

The hell it did. He wrapped his arms around Scarlett. "Trust me, she's better than any pain medicine." He'd always gotten a little drunk on Scarlett.

Scarlett smiled down at him. "I can wait," she murmured. "Because we will have plenty of time."

He wanted forever with her.

Ava slipped around the nurse and into Grant's room. Her eyes lit up when she saw him. "You look so much better!" She ran toward him and gave him a big hug. "I thought I was going to lose you," she whispered. "Just like..."

She stopped, but he knew exactly what she'd been going to say.

Our parents.

"I'm not going anyplace," he promised her.

Scarlett cleared her throat. "I think...I need to go downstairs for a bit, anyway, so you two should probably have some private time."

He didn't want her leaving. Grant shook his head.

"I have to meet my lawyer." Her smile flashed. "I'll be back before you know I'm gone." She eased toward the door.

As she stood near his bed, Ava was shifting nervously from foot to foot. "I—I didn't mean to interrupt you two."

He caught his sister's hand in his.

"You didn't," Scarlett assured her.

The nurse was bustling around the room, checking Grant's vitals and going over his chart.

"I'll be back soon," Scarlett told Grant as her eyes met his.

"Scarlett—"

She was gone. He *hated* that bed right then. Hated the pain that still left him weak.

She'll be back.

The hope she'd given him was just so new and fresh, and until the threats against her were gone, Grant wanted Scarlett close.

The nurse slipped from the room, too.

He turned his head and saw that Ava was watching him, her gaze nervous.

She took a deep breath. "Is what happened to you… is it related to our parents?"

That question gave him pause. He'd just assumed the attack was tied to Scarlett, but he didn't have proof of that. "I don't know."

Ava backed up a step. "I'm always worried about that, always been afraid that they'll come back." She raked a hand through her hair. "Years later, and I still jump when I hear sounds in the night. Ridiculous, isn't it?"

"No." He didn't think anything about his sister was ridiculous.

"I want to be stronger." Her hands were small fists in front of her. "I will be stronger."

He reached out and caught one of those fists in his hand. "You already are strong, sis." But she'd never seen herself that way. She'd ridden on horseback in the black of night, she'd gone for help—but she saw herself as the coward who'd fled and left her parents to die.

"If I'd been stronger, I could have saved them."

He gave a sharp, negative shake of his head. "Their deaths aren't on you."

"Then why do I always feel like they are?"

Survivor's guilt. He knew exactly why she couldn't let go.

"They're not on you," he said again, willing her to believe him. "And one day, you will stop being afraid. You'll be able to sleep at night without the nightmares coming back. You'll see what I see—just how strong you really are." His fingers tightened on hers.

"Promise?" she asked, and she reminded him so much of the girl she'd been. Before monsters had wrecked her life.

"I swear it."

SCARLETT STEPPED AWAY from Grant's door. A uniformed cop stood to the right of it, and Brodie was propped against the wall on the left.

Grant's brother frowned when he saw her heading toward the elevators. "What's the rush, Scarlett?"

"I'm meeting my lawyer." She pressed the down button on the control panel. "He said that the case is going to be dismissed." The doors opened right then—talk about perfect timing.

"Wait, and I can go with you—"

But she shook her head. "I'm not leaving the hospital. Pierce is coming here. I'm just meeting him downstairs."

She walked into the elevator, and pretty much slammed into Davis.

He caught her shoulders.

"Sorry," she muttered. She'd been so distracted she hadn't been paying enough attention. Scarlett felt red stain her cheeks. She pulled back from him, trying to give him room to leave the elevator.

But he wasn't moving. He was studying her with worried eyes. Why did all the McGuire brothers have to look so cautious all the time?

"She's going to meet her lawyer."

Her head snapped around. Brodie had put his hands on the elevator's doors to keep them open. "Give her an escort, man."

Davis nodded. Brodie eased back and the doors started to close.

"This isn't necessary," Scarlett rushed to assure him. "I'm just going downstairs. I'll be perfectly fine." She didn't need constant protection.

"Better safe," Davis murmured.

Than sorry.

Her lips tightened just as her phone rang. She pulled it out, recognizing Pierce's number on the screen. Scarlett lifted the phone to her ear. "Pierce, are you already in the lobby?" Talk about fast.

"No…parking garage…" Static crackled over the line. "DA's here…level four. Couldn't park out front because two ambulances were blocking that entrance."

She leaned forward and pressed the button for the parking garage on level four. "I'm on my way there. Give me just a few moments." Then they could sign the paperwork together. She ended the call. Tapped her foot.

And was far too conscious of Davis's gaze on her.

The doors opened seconds later. The cavernous parking garage waited. She stepped forward, but Davis caught her arm and pulled her right back. "Hold on," he said, frowning as he looked out into that parking garage. "This…this setup doesn't feel right to me."

"Scarlett?" Pierce called her name as he appeared before them. He smiled at her. He was holding his briefcase. "It's over," he told her, that smile spreading even more. "You're clear."

Scarlett tried to shrug free from Davis's hold.

Pierce fumbled with his briefcase. His gloved fingers slid over the rich leather. Scarlett left the elevator, with Davis close at her side.

"I've got the papers in here," the lawyer said, panting a bit. "Got them—"

He pulled out a gun.

Davis grabbed Scarlett and jerked her to the side even as a shot rang out. But that bullet didn't hit her.

Pierce had been aiming for Davis. The bullet slammed into his shoulder and he staggered back.

Pierce lifted the weapon, aiming again.

And Davis lunged at him in a tackle. They went down together in a crush of bodies.

Gunfire thundered again. In that echoing garage, it sounded like a car backfiring.

Davis slumped to the side. Scarlett grabbed for him, flipping him over, and sucked in a horrified breath when she saw the blood oozing from his chest. "Davis!"

"You should have come alone." Pierce was on his feet again. He put the gun to her head. "Now get away from him."

Davis's eyes were open. On her.

"Get away, or I will shoot him again. This time that bullet will go straight into his heart. I missed then…at least, I think I missed…"

Davis's breath heaved out in pain-filled gasps.

"Move away or he's dead."

Scarlett rose to her feet.

"I hate using guns," Pierce muttered. He glanced down at his gloved hand as he held the weapon. "Seems too rough. So impersonal." He grabbed her arm and yanked her against him. "Now, a knife, oh, but that's a different matter. You can feel it when the knife slices deep."

This wasn't happening. "Why?" He was her lawyer, for goodness sake! He'd been Eric's friend. He helped people!

"Because it was all your fault, Scarlett." Pierce was dragging her away then, pulling her deeper into the shadows of the garage. "Everything that happened to him... your fault. And it's time you paid for what you did."

He popped the trunk on his car. "Get in."

She shook her head. If she got into that trunk, she was dead. Scarlett knew that with utter certainty. "No."

Why wasn't anyone else in that parking garage? *Why?*

"Get. In!" he ordered.

She shook her head, and then attacked. She hit him, slamming out with her fists and kicking. Her nails sliced down his face. *Got your DNA, jerk.* No matter what else happened, she'd leave her mark on him.

He snarled when her knee hit his groin, and Scarlett leaped away then, thinking she might have time to get to cover before—

He grabbed a fistful of her hair and yanked her back toward him. She tried to resist, but he brought up the butt of his weapon and slammed it into her head.

For a moment, the world seemed to spin around her. No, no, *she* was spinning, because he'd lifted her up and he was dumping her into the trunk.

"No!" Scarlett screamed, even as dizziness hit her as hard as that gun had. "Don't!" Her hands flew up.

But he slammed the trunk with such force that her right wrist snapped.

Scarlett screamed again. She kept screaming, over and over, even as she felt the car begin to move.

She was still screaming when he drove away.

Chapter Thirteen

"Scarlett should have been back by now." Grant frowned at the clock that hung on his wall. She'd been gone for nearly thirty minutes.

Why wasn't she back?

"She's probably just still talking to her lawyer," Ava said, giving a little nod. "Don't worry, I'm sure she'll be back up here soon."

He glanced at the window. Tension had been growing within him with every moment that passed. His instincts, kicking in again…or just his overprotective nature?

He reached for the phone on the bedside. Dialed Scarlett's number. Fine, he was overprotective. After everything they'd been through, he had that right, didn't he?

The phone rang once, twice…

HER PHONE WAS RINGING.

Scarlett grabbed for the cell. She'd tried using it before. Again and again—but there had been no service. No service! She'd used the light app on her phone to try and find a weapon in that trunk, but Pierce had stripped the small space of anything useful.

He'd planned this.

Now the phone was working—yes! "Help me!" Scarlett cried as she fumbled with that phone. She didn't know who the caller was, but that didn't matter. "Please, help me!"

"Scarlett?" It was Grant's shocked voice.

"Please…" She clutched the phone desperately. "Pierce took me. He…he shot Davis."

Static crackled over the line, and she was afraid that she was about to lose service again.

"What?" Fury broke through Grant's shock. "Where are you? Where is my brother?"

"Davis is in the parking garage…level four." The lowest level. The one that she now realized was rarely used. *Pierce had known exactly how to isolate me.* "Help him! He was…he was alive." And her words were a tangled mess. "When we left…"

"Where are you?"

"His trunk." Her head was throbbing again. It kept doing that…and Scarlett thought she might have passed out. Once? Twice? She had a giant knot on her skull, one that still bled. "Get the cops…to find his car…"

But Grant didn't respond.

"Grant?" she whispered. "Grant?" Scarlett screamed.

Then she looked at the phone. In the dark, she could see the glowing screen so clearly.

No service.

"SCARLETT?" GRANT ROARED.

But she was gone.

He leaped from the bed. Yanked the IV out of his hand. Nearly slammed facedown on the floor.

But Ava grabbed him. "Grant? Grant, what's wrong?"

The door flew open. Brodie and a uniformed cop rushed inside.

"Scarlett." Saying her name had his heart nearly

ripping out of his chest. "Her lawyer—he's the one we're after! He took her!"

Ava's face went slack with horror and shock.

"He shot…Davis…"

Brodie grabbed Grant. "I sent Davis down with Scarlett!"

"Parking garage," Grant said, gritting his teeth against the pain. He could feel the stitches pulling along his side. He didn't care if he broke every single one of them. "Level four. Get him."

Brodie raced out of the room.

"Grant, please, get back in bed," Ava whispered.

Hell, no. He grabbed for clothes. Managed to mostly get dressed. The cop was calling for backup. Shouting and asking Grant to tell him more about—

"Pierce Jennings. Thirty-five, six foot two. Black hair, green eyes. He was her *lawyer*," Grant snarled as he made his staggering way to the door. "Get an APB out for him. And try to track Scarlett's phone." He rattled off her cell number. "We have to find them."

Terror held him in a desperate grip.

Ava stepped in front of him. "You can't leave. Grant, you can barely stand up!"

He'd crawl after her if he had to do it. "She needs… me," he managed to gasp. "I won't…live…without her."

His sister swallowed, her eyes widening with realization. "You love her that much?"

More than anything.

Ava came closer to him. She slid his arm around her shoulders. "Then let's find her," she said, her voice growing stronger. "Let's find her."

SHE TRIED TO call Grant again and again, but the phone wouldn't work. She'd searched for the trunk release lever.

All American cars made after 2002 had trunk release levers—she knew that. But there was no sign of the glow-in-the-dark handle near the latch. She searched for a toggle switch or even a button—one that didn't glow—but there was nothing there.

Had Pierce removed the trunk release lever?

No doubt, damn him.

So she twisted her body and started fighting with the seats. If she could push them down or pry them loose enough to shove them out of her way, she'd escape into the backseat. She'd attack Pierce—stop him somehow.

Her right wrist kept throbbing as she moved, and Scarlett knew it was broken. But a broken wrist was the least of her worries. When Pierce got her to whatever destination he had in mind—

He'll kill me.

But she knew it wouldn't be an easy death. Because if he'd wanted fast and easy, he could have just shot her in that parking garage. The same way he'd shot Davis.

Be alive, Davis. Please! Grant would get him help. She knew it with utter certainty. *If* Davis was still alive.

The car seemed to slow down.

No…

And then the vehicle stopped.

"You should be in bed!" Shayne glowered at Grant. "What the hell are you thinking?"

"I'm thinking that Scarlett needs me, and I'll be damned if I leave her alone with him."

He could feel blood oozing on his side. Some of the stitches had already given way. The others wouldn't be far behind.

Shayne growled. "Fine. Damn fool!" He ran a hand through his already tousled hair. "We've got the video surveillance feeds running here, but they're no use—at least, not from the fourth garage level. Pierce blacked them out."

They were in the guards' station at the hospital. Davis was in surgery. Brodie had found him. He was alive, thank God, and the doctors were working frantically to patch him up.

The bullet didn't hit his heart. Those had been Brodie's gruff words.

Then Brodie hadn't spoken again. Just joined the swarm in the guards' office as the police launched their search.

"There…there!" Excitement kicked in Shayne's voice as he pointed to one of the monitors. "That's Pierce's car leaving the hospital at 11:04."

Too long ago. "The APB," Grant snapped at him. "Why haven't your officers found him?"

"Because he's probably too good at hiding." Shayne was sweating. "But we have a GPS trace working on her phone now. If Scarlett comes within range again for us, then we'll have them."

"We don't have this time to kill," Grant retorted desperately. They couldn't just wait and hope to get lucky. "He's hurting her."

Killing her?

The door flew open then. Mac stood in the entrance, chest heaving. "Pierce has got property just twenty miles from the McGuire ranch. Isolated, unused from what I can tell…"

"A perfect kill spot." Brodie's voice.

Grant wished his other brother had stayed silent.

"The black SUV came from that area. I think he was out there," Mac continued, "waiting for you. Waiting to attack."

Did you want me out of the way so you could get to Scarlett?

"I've got a chopper on standby," Shayne said.

Hell, yes. "Then let's get that bird in the air!" Grant took a step forward. Staggered.

Brodie grabbed him. "You can't do this." His eyes glinted. "I'll go. I will kill that SOB for you."

Grant believed him. There was no mistaking his brother's fury. Brodie's twin had been attacked, left for dead. Brodie would not rest until he'd gotten his vengeance.

But...it was about more than vengeance. *Scarlett is mine.* "I'm going for her."

Brodie gave a grim nod. "How big is this chopper?"

They were *all* going for her.

SCARLETT POSITIONED HERSELF so that she was ready for Pierce. When that trunk opened, she shot her legs out, catching him in the stomach. He grunted and stumbled back, and she jumped from the vehicle. Her legs pistoned as she ran, pushing forward as fast as she could.

He was behind her, yelling, and she expected to feel the impact of a bullet hitting her at any moment.

Instead, he tackled her. They slammed into the ground. Her face hit the dirt and her knee struck a big rock.

He flipped her over and pressed a knife to her throat.

She realized then why he hadn't fired at her. He'd switched to his *personal* weapon.

"Why do you fight so hard," he panted, "when you know there's no escape?"

"Why are you doing this?" Scarlett shouted right back.

He blinked, seeming to be caught off guard by the question. "Do you truly destroy so many lives that you can't remember?"

Insane. "I haven't destroyed anyone's life! I haven't—"

"Ian."

The name was the last one she expected to hear then. "I haven't see Ian in years." *Ian is dead.* Grant had told her that.

Pierce's blade pricked against her throat. He'd been the man in her condo. The one who'd come to kill her.

"Of course you haven't seen him. It's not easy to see the dead." Her lawyer rose, dragging her up with him. "You killed him."

"No, I didn't!" She'd gotten as far from that guy as she could. She hadn't even known about his death until yesterday.

"You ruined his life…crash and burn…and you never looked back." Pierce was hauling her toward a small run-down cabin as he talked, and he never once took the knife away from her throat. "I guess that's what you do, isn't it? You use your lovers. Wreck them. And you never glance back to see what you've done."

"Ian attacked me! He shoved me down a flight of stairs!"

"You fell," he said flatly. "Then you wouldn't let go, would you? You had to contact his parents. Had to send them those damn pictures of you—and they cut him off!"

Her breath caught in her throat. "Who was Ian to you?"

This nightmare…it was all tied to a man she'd known years ago?

"My stepbrother. I never saw him as much as I wanted, not after my father left us and remarried for a third time." Pierce kicked open the door of the cabin. Shoved her inside. "Just a few times a year, that's when my father would call me over, and Ian would be there. I knew it was my job to help Ian. To protect him."

"Ian hurt me." Scarlett's voice was strangely calm.

Odd, when she was shaking so much on the inside. "I didn't destroy his life. I just wanted him out of *my* life!"

"You started the accusations." The words were feverish. "You ruined his reputation!"

Bull. No one had believed her at their university.

"He had to leave in disgrace. First you…then the others, they all started accusing him."

The others?

Pierce's breath heaved out as he forced her into a nearby chair. Then he tied her hands behind her.

With a sinking heart, Scarlett realized just how thoroughly he'd planned her abduction—and murder.

"You think I haven't seen innocent men get framed before? I see it every day." His laughter was cold. Cruel. "After all this time, I learned how to use the system."

"You learned how to set me up," she whispered.

He yanked on the ropes, and they cut into her skin. Agony shot up from her broken wrist.

"You were supposed to go to prison. That's where Ian was when he died. His life, your life. An even balance."

"I didn't destroy Ian." She wouldn't give in to this jerk. "He did that to himself."

Pierce lunged at her, and Scarlett expected to feel the knife drive into her chest.

Grant's image flashed through her mind. A sob built in her throat.

But the knife didn't drive into her. Her attacker stilled, his eyes burning with emotion. "I've seen innocent men spend their lives in jail. I've seen the guilty walk free. I've *let* the guilty walk." He shook his head. "No more. There has to be a judgment. No. More!"

"I didn't send Ian to jail!" She'd tried. "I wasn't the one—"

"Ian's dead." He said it simply. Chillingly. "I told you, there has to be a judgment."

Goose bumps rose onto her arms. "When did Ian die?"

"Last year…last year…right before you walked into that damn party here in Austin. You were on Eric's arm, smiling your fake smile, and I remembered you. I remembered what Ian told me about you." Spittle flew from the lawyer's mouth. "I tried to warn Eric about you. That you were trouble. That you cheated. Lied—"

Understanding filled her. Too late. "That was why he hired Louis East."

Pierce smiled. "And I'm the one who told Justin that he had to be wary of you. That you were out to cut him from his brother's life. The bond between brothers…it should be unbreakable."

When she thought of a bond between brothers, she didn't think of Pierce and his twisted connection to Ian. She thought of Grant. The McGuire family. "Yes," she said, breath rushing out. "It should be."

"I even went to Justin when he was in lockup at the police station. Told him that he had to act, or you'd take away his inheritance—everything that Eric had left. I warned Justin that you weren't done with him yet. That you'd confessed to me that you killed Eric." He laughed. "He was so easy to aim and use. After our little talk, I knew he'd go after you—or Grant McGuire."

"I didn't kill anyone," she said, giving a hard shake of her head. "You did, and the cops will realize it! They'll find footage of you at that hospital. I—I told Grant that you had me! I—"

He'd stilled. "What did you do?" Then his face twisted with rage. "Your phone! Your damn phone!" His hands flew over her, and he grabbed for the cell in her pocket. "I forgot the damn phone!"

"Yes, you did." He didn't know she hadn't been able to get service for long. "The cops know everything. They're coming after you."

He whirled away from her. Started pacing. "They weren't going to find your body. Without a body…prosecuting is nearly impossible. I was going to say you ran away, fled because you feared being sent to jail—"

He was crazy. "You shot Davis! How were you going to explain *that*?" She yanked at the ropes. There was no give to them at all.

"He shouldn't have been with you." Pierce's shoulders were stiff, his fingers white as they gripped the knife. "You should have come alone to meet me, and then I never would have shot him. He wasn't part of my plan."

"Your plan is insane! You aren't getting away with this!"

He faced her once more. His brows lowered. "Maybe you shot Davis. Maybe he found out that you'd hired someone to try and kill Grant…" Pierce nodded. "Yes, that could work. You—you're a black widow, that's what you are. The press will have a field day. They'll love—"

"You're the killer! You're the one who is twisted!" She jerked hard against the bonds. The chair rocked. "Everything that has happened…it is on you!"

Then she heard a faint sound. A whirring in the distance. Louder than wind, stronger.

Pierce jerked, and she knew he'd heard that sound, too.

"What the hell is that?" he demanded.

She jerked once more on the ropes. The chair rocked, then toppled. She fell to the floor with a loud thump. Dust and dirt flew around her, and some of the wooden floor slats broke away as the legs of the chair crashed into them.

Pierce whirled back toward her.

The whirring grew louder. Closer.

And she knew exactly what that sound was. A helicopter…closing in.

Coming…for her?

"THE CABIN'S DOWN THERE!" Grant shouted.

The pilot had already seen it and was bringing the bird around for a landing. They'd flown as fast as possible to get out here, and every moment had taken *too long* for Grant. He had to get to Scarlett.

Before it was too late.

Mac and Brodie were both silent in that chopper.

Shayne was barking orders, getting officers to meet them on the ground, but those ground forces wouldn't be able to arrive as quickly as the helicopter.

"I see his car," Grant said when the lights from the aircraft swept the scene. The car's trunk hung open. "He's there!" The cabin was dark, and he couldn't see Pierce or Scarlett, but they had to be inside.

The chopper lowered toward the ground. Grant jerked free of his harness. He shoved aside his headset. The force of the helicopter's blades sent dust blowing and had the trees billowing.

As soon as the bird touched down, Grant leaped outside. He was bleeding, he knew. Could feel the blood-soaked shirt clinging to him. More stitches had torn, and it was all he could do to keep upright, but there was no way he would fall. No way.

Scarlett was too close.

Brodie and Mac were right beside him as they ran for the cabin. Shayne had a weapon—and so did the McGuire brothers. They were all licensed to carry the guns, and they knew better than to go into a situation like this unarmed.

"Pierce Jennings!" Shayne shouted. "Let the woman go and come out with your hands up!"

Or we'll be coming in...and ripping you apart.

Fury and fear gave Grant strength as the adrenaline pounded through him. He would be getting Scarlett back. No matter what he had to do.

Hold on, baby. Hold on.

THE BROKEN WOOD from the floor sliced across Scarlett's arms. The back of the chair had cracked, and another hard yank from her had the chair splintering even more. She twisted her body and managed to almost get free—

"Pierce Jennings! Let the woman go and come out with your hands up!"

Her breath rushed out.

"No." Pierce shook his head. "No, this isn't how it's supposed to be." He rushed toward the grime-covered window. Tried to peer outside. "They weren't supposed to be here!"

"They are here," she told him, panting. "And they are going to come through that door any second. Give up now, and you can live."

"In prison…"

Where else did he think he'd be living? The Caymans?

"Give up now!" Scarlett told him frantically.

The ropes had finally slipped off.

"I won't go to jail. I won't be like Ian."

Too late, buddy. You already are.

"I hand out the judgment." He whirled from the window. Stared at her with deadly intent. "This will be for Ian, just like the others…"

He ran toward her. He lifted up the knife.

"No!" Scarlett screamed. Her hands flew out, hitting the broken wood of the floor as she tried to surge up and—

Her fingers closed around something hard. Cold. Metal? No, no it was—

He swiped out with his knife.

WHEN GRANT HEARD Scarlett's scream, something in him broke. He lunged past the others. Knocked in that front door.

The scene froze before him—Pierce, swinging down with his knife. Scarlett, crouched on the floor. He knew in a flash that Pierce intended to kill Scarlett. Right then.

"Get away from her!" Grant roared as he flew across the room.

Gunfire exploded.

Pierce staggered back.

Gunfire?

The lawyer shook his head and tried to lunge toward Scarlett once more. Not happening. Grant tackled the guy. They hit the floor with a jarring impact. Grant felt more of his stitches tear away, but he was numb to any pain. Pierce tried to lift up his knife, slicing toward Grant's throat.

"No." Grant caught Pierce's wrist in a steely grip.

Footsteps pounded behind him.

"Drop the weapon!" Shayne shouted.

Pierce glared at Grant. "I'll kill you…that will be punishment…enough."

Grant rolled them, yanked down on the lawyer's wrist—and shoved the man's own knife into Pierce's heart.

"No," Grant told him flatly as he stared into his shocked eyes. "I'll kill *you*."

Pierce's breath rasped out. His fingers slid away from the knife.

Grant didn't let the guy go. Not yet. Not...

Pierce's eyes began to sag shut.

"For *my* brother," Grant said. "And for Scarlett."

Then he pushed away from the man. Tried to stand... but, hell, Grant's strength was fading.

The blood on the floor wasn't just Pierce's. His own blood was pumping out of him.

"The McGuire Brothers," Shayne whispered. "*Damn*, you play for keeps."

No, they didn't play at all.

Scarlett locked her arms around Grant.

He held her as tightly as he could.

"Uh, Scarlett..." Brodie's voice was low, "How about you drop that gun now? We've got him. That fellow isn't a threat to anyone now."

Scarlett had been the one to shoot Pierce. Grant felt her nod, and then heard the gun clatter as she dropped it.

He looked over her shoulder. Shayne had bent beside Pierce. The cop glared down at the lawyer. "So many lives...for what?"

"Revenge," Scarlett whispered.

Grant's arms began to slide down her body.

"That his gun you used?" Brodie approached her slowly. "They'll need it for evidence."

Backup would be arriving. Medics. Grant could use those medics. "Are you hurt?" he asked Scarlett. His voice slurred.

"Doesn't matter," she whispered back as she kissed him. "Doesn't matter now—it's over!"

Yes, it was.

"And it's not his gun," Scarlett muttered. "Or maybe

it is, I don't know. The floor broke, and two guns were under the slats. I—I grabbed one. Fired."

The room began to whirl around Grant. "Scarlett." Saying her name was an effort, but she needed to hear this.

His body slumped against her.

"Grant? Grant!"

"Love you…and I'm not…going anywhere…" His breath rushed out. "Just a scratch…"

"Get him back to the chopper!" Shayne bellowed.

Grant kept staring into Scarlett's eyes. *"Got you."* He hadn't been about to let her go. "Love…you…"

When he went to hit the floor, his brother hauled him upright.

"Just…" Grant said again, "a scratch…"

SCARLETT WAS AT Grant's bedside once more. Her wrist was in a cast, and her head ached only a little.

It was her heart that hurt the most.

"You should have made him stay here," Scarlett said. She'd said the same words about twenty times already.

Mac grunted from his post behind her. "Right. Because the guy *always* listens to someone else's orders."

"He was too weak." She'd never forget the sight of him breaking down that door. "Too hurt."

"Grant would have bled out before he let anything happen to you." Mac's voice was deep, quiet. "You think I was going to be dumb enough to stand between that man and what he wanted most?"

He was what she wanted, too.

Her fingers brushed back his hair. "Grant." She didn't know if he could hear her, but she needed to say this. "Stop risking your life for me. If we're going to be together, you *can't* keep doing this."

His eyelashes flickered.

Her gaze narrowed.

She wondered just how long he'd been awake.

"Grant?"

His eyes opened. That green gaze was fully aware. "Can't...make promises."

Her breath rushed out.

"I'd risk...anything...for you."

And she'd risk anything for him.

"Love you...Scarlett."

She pressed her lips to his. "And I love you, Grant." It seemed as if she always had.

And she always would.

His lips curved into a faint smile.

In that moment, Scarlett knew that the past was over for them. The fear was gone. It was time for them to look toward the future.

A new life.

Hope.

The love that would see them through all the days ahead.

His fingers curled around hers. "Told you," he whispered. "It was just a scratch."

She kissed him again.

Epilogue

It was too soon for marriage. Grant knew he needed to give Scarlett more time. He wanted to court the woman. Wanted to treat her like the damn precious thing that she was.

He wanted to show her how good their life could be together.

He also didn't want to be hobbling down the aisle.

He winced as his stitches—another new set—pulled when he stood.

He'd been going stir-crazy in that hospital. He'd needed to get out. Return to work. Start getting his life back to normal. A life that now included Scarlett.

So he'd bought a ring for her. And that ring was burning a hole in his pocket. He'd wait until the time was right.

Then he'd get down on his knees for her.

A knock sounded at his office door. Frowning, Grant glanced up as his assistant, Madison, poked her head inside.

"Detective Townsend is here to see you, Grant."

He nodded. "Send him in." He knew Shayne had been tying up all the loose ends that Pierce Jennings had left behind. Every time Grant thought of that SOB, fury burned within him.

Pierce had truly been as twisted as Ian. No, he'd been worse. Because Pierce had actually thought what he was doing was justified. That it was somehow okay to kill for vengeance.

Shayne's face was tense when he strode into Grant's office. The detective shut the door. Didn't sit down.

Grant's brows climbed. "What is it?"

Shayne opened his mouth to reply, then stopped.

Grant tensed. It wasn't like the cop to hesitate. "Shayne?"

"You're...happy now, right?"

What the hell kind of question was that?

"You love Scarlett, and you're planning for the future."

The ring weighed heavily in his pocket.

"I want you to keep thinking of her," Shayne said slowly, "and of your future. Think about the good things that you have going for you."

Grant rose and advanced on his friend. "What's happening?"

"Sometimes, you think the past is over. Dead and gone." Shayne's gaze was shuttered. "Then something comes along and wrecks your world. It changes... *everything.*"

"Tell me why you're here." It was a demand.

Shayne swallowed. "Those two guns found at Pierce's cabin...underneath that old floor..."

Grant's gut twisted as a premonition seemed to sweep over him.

"They'd been used before. The bullet that Scarlett fired at Pierce was a match for another case. A cold case."

Grant couldn't have moved then if his life depended on it.

"Those were the weapons used to kill your parents."

The past is never dead and gone.

The door opened behind Shayne. Brodie strode inside. His gaze darted from the cop to his battle-tense brother.

Brodie's face hardened instantly. "What's happening?"

Grant forced himself to take a slow, deep breath. This was the break they'd needed. This was the turning point for them. They wouldn't get vengeance. They weren't looking for twisted punishment. They *weren't* like Pierce.

They wanted justice. They would have it. The men who'd killed their parents would spend the rest of their lives in a jail cell.

"Grant…" Brodie demanded. "Tell me what is happening here!"

He nodded. "The McGuires are going hunting."

* * * * *

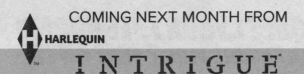

REQUEST YOUR FREE BOOKS!
2 FREE NOVELS PLUS 2 FREE GIFTS!

HARLEQUIN

INTRIGUE

BREATHTAKING ROMANTIC SUSPENSE

YES! Please send me 2 FREE Harlequin Intrigue® novels and my 2 FREE gifts (gifts are worth about $10). After receiving them, if I don't wish to receive any more books, I can return the shipping statement marked "cancel." If I don't cancel, I will receive 6 brand-new novels every month and be billed just $4.74 per book in the U.S. or $5.24 per book in Canada. That's a savings of at least 14% off the cover price! It's quite a bargain! Shipping and handling is just 50¢ per book in the U.S. and 75¢ per book in Canada.* I understand that accepting the 2 free books and gifts places me under no obligation to buy anything. I can always return a shipment and cancel at any time. Even if I never buy another book, the two free books and gifts are mine to keep forever.

182/382 HDN F42N

Name _____ (PLEASE PRINT) _____

Address _____ Apt. #

City _____ State/Prov. _____ Zip/Postal Code

Signature (if under 18, a parent or guardian must sign)

Mail to the **Harlequin® Reader Service:**
IN U.S.A.: P.O. Box 1867, Buffalo, NY 14240-1867
IN CANADA: P.O. Box 609, Fort Erie, Ontario L2A 5X3
**Are you a subscriber to Harlequin Intrigue books
and want to receive the larger-print edition?
Call 1-800-873-8635 or visit www.ReaderService.com.**

* Terms and prices subject to change without notice. Prices do not include applicable taxes. Sales tax applicable in N.Y. Canadian residents will be charged applicable taxes. Offer not valid in Quebec. This offer is limited to one order per household. Not valid for current subscribers to Harlequin Intrigue books. All orders subject to credit approval. Credit or debit balances in a customer's account(s) may be offset by any other outstanding balance owed by or to the customer. Please allow 4 to 6 weeks for delivery. Offer available while quantities last.

Your Privacy—The Harlequin® Reader Service is committed to protecting your privacy. Our Privacy Policy is available online at www.ReaderService.com or upon request from the Harlequin Reader Service.

We make a portion of our mailing list available to reputable third parties that offer products we believe may interest you. If you prefer that we not exchange your name with third parties, or if you wish to clarify or modify your communication preferences, please visit us at www.ReaderService.com/consumerchoice or write to us at Harlequin Reader Service Preference Service, P.O. Box 9062, Buffalo, NY 14269. Include your complete name and address.

HI13R

*A Texas deputy steps in to protect a vulnerable witness,
even though she could send his own father to jail...*

"You know that I'm staying here with you tonight, right,"
Colt said when he pulled to a stop in front of her house.

Elise was certain that wasn't a question, and she wanted
to insist his babysitting her wasn't necessary.

But she was afraid that it was.

Because someone wanted her dead. Had even sent
someone to end her life. And that someone had nearly
succeeded.

She'd hoped the bone-deep exhaustion would tamp
down the fear. It didn't. She was feeling both fear and
fatigue, and that wasn't a good mix.

Nor was having Colt around.

However, the alternative was her being alone in her
house that was miles from town or her nearest neighbor.
And for just the rest of the night, she wasn't ready for
the alone part. In the morning though, she would have to
do something to remedy it. Something that didn't include
Colt and her under the same roof.

For now though, that was exactly what was about to
happen.

They got out of his truck, the sleet still spitting at them,
and the air so bitterly cold that it burned her lungs with
each breath she took. Elise's hands were still shaking,
and when she tried to unlock the front door of her house,
she dropped the gob of keys, the metal sound clattering

onto the weathered wood porch. Colt reached for them at the same time she did, and their heads ended up colliding.

Right on her stitches.

The pain shot through her, and even though Elise tried to choke back the groan, she didn't quite succeed.

"Sorry." Colt cursed and snatched the keys from her to unlock the door. He definitely wasn't shaking.

"Wait here," he ordered the moment they stepped into the living room. He shut the door, gave her a stay-put warning glance and drew his gun before he started looking around.

Only then did Elise realize that someone—another hit man maybe—could be already hiding inside. Waiting to kill her.

Sweet heaven.

When was this going to end?

As the threats to Elise Nichols escalate, so does the tension between her and sexy cowboy Colt McKinnon!

Don't miss their heart-stopping story when
THE DEPUTY'S REDEMPTION,
part of USA TODAY bestselling author
Delores Fossen's SWEETWATER RANCH miniseries,
goes on sale in March 2015.

HARLEQUIN®
A *Romance* FOR EVERY MOOD™

Love the Harlequin book you just read?

Your opinion matters.

Review this book on your favorite
book site, review site, blog or your own
social media properties and share
your opinion with other readers!

Be sure to connect with us at:
Harlequin.com/Newsletters
Facebook.com/HarlequinBooks
Twitter.com/HarlequinBooks